A Voice in the Tower

THE OLD TALES

C.H. LYN

Horizon Publishing

Also by C.H. Lyn

The Old Tales

Song of the Deep

The Abredea Series

Hope and Lies

Truth and Fury

Miss Belle's Travel Guides

Lacey Goes to Tokyo

Damen Goes to Peru

Spooky Cat Stories

Spooky Cat

One Hell of a Road Trip

Other Works

Love is Murder

Contents

Dedication   VIII

The Old Tales Map   IX

1. What's in a Name?   1

2. Impossible   6

3. Not a Witch   13

4. Not Quite Born for the Role   20

5. Greggory the Mouse   27

6. Beans   33

7. Small Victories   38

8. Heard   42

9. Lost Names   48

10. A Maid and an Embrace   53

11. Wishing   58

12. Brotherly Conversations   63

13. A Charming Village   70

14. A Melancholy Trek   77

15. An Ocean Apart   83

16. Silver Spoon   88

17. The Great Cleanse   96

18. The Tower   101

19. This I Vow   106

20. Message in a Bone   112

21. Fear and Fury   117

22. Righting Wrongs   120

23. Splinters in the Dark   126

24. Nearly There   131

25. An Illusion   135

26. Hear the Difference   139

27. Blood on the Grass   139

28. Watching, Wishing, Wanting   139

29. Advice of a Sea Witch   139

30. Brothers   139

Acknowledgements   139

Dedication

Kels, you're a princess.
Thank you.

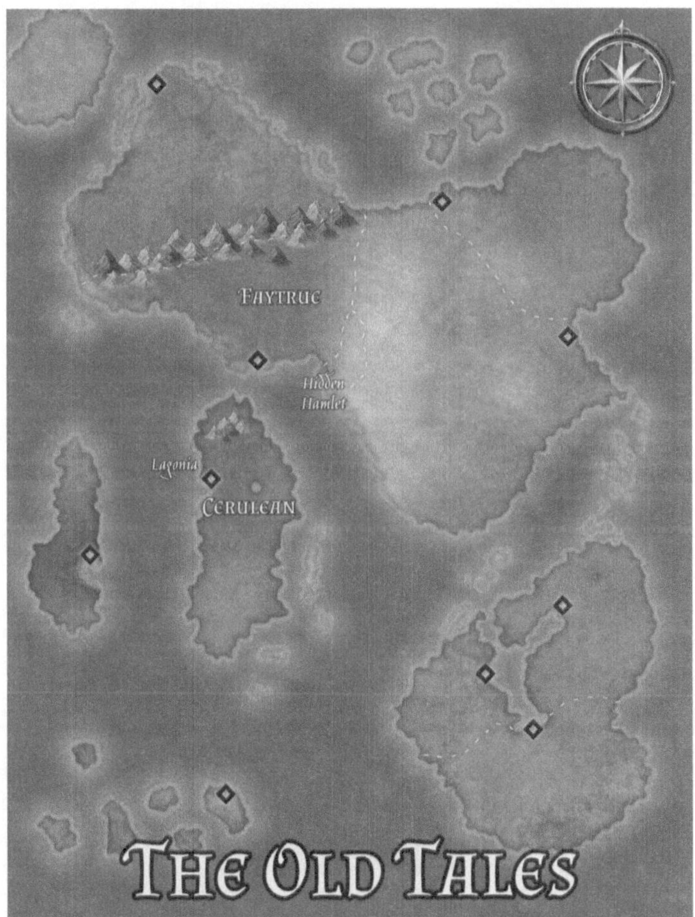

THE OLD TALES

Chapter One

What's in a Name?

Rivanissee Stephanie Claire Von Montague was not overly fond of her name. Still, she could have her sister's name which was nearly twice as long and had gotten "Ralpert" thrown on the end after her recent wedding.

No, Riva knew she was lucky with her second child name. She'd gladly take Rivanissee over being crown princess any day of the week.

She did have to admit, she thought as she hurried down a servant's hall to the kitchen, it was entirely likely that her older sister got to sleep in every morning. Even with a new husband and a child on the way.

There were perks of being first in line to the throne after all.

Riva was second in line, and the gap between the two had been as wide as a gorge since the day she'd been born. It didn't help that their mother had died shortly after. There was no one to bring them together save their father, and a king had more important business than caring for his children.

Riva shook her head to clear it of such thoughts. They'd only resurfaced with her sister's wedding, an event that had sparked an argument between the two of them about love, duty, and each's dedication to the wellbeing of their kingdom.

With a hand on the door to the kitchen, Riva inhaled, adjusted her skirts, and pushed it open.

"Princess!" A child of nearly eight scurried toward her through the throng and bustle of a palace kitchen just before dawn.

"Benji." Riva grinned down at him. The scents and sounds here calmed her. "You helping your mum this morning?"

"Tryin' to," Benji said with a moan. "But she won't let me near the chickens after last time."

Riva stifled a laugh as Benji's mother, a fierce, stout redhead, raised an eyebrow from her usual place by the stove. Marian was a gruff woman. She was rarely seen without her apron and heavy wooden spoon. Though her husband had passed in the war when Benji was little, she had yet to remarry. Each time Riva broached the topic of the handsome middle-aged man who ran the stables, Marian insisted that there was too much to do and romance would only get in the way.

"I don't need yeh cracking half the king's breakfast before I've had a chance to make it," Marian scolded.

When Benji turned his big eyes and pouting lips on her, she broke into a laugh.

"If the princess goes with you."

Benji turned to Riva, who was also chuckling at his antics.

She grabbed a basket from the counter. "Let's go then."

"Get them back here quick," Marian called after them. "His Majesty has an early meeting today."

Riva wondered briefly who her father was to meet with before becoming entirely distracted by Benji's leaps and bounds through the back kitchen door into the courtyard.

She took her braids, both tightly wound and still dangling past her waist, and knotted them into a bun at the base of her neck.

As Benji hurried toward the chicken coop, Riva took a bag of grain from a hook and began clucking at the birds to draw them away for breakfast. She scattered the meal on the dusty cobblestone ground, enjoying the crisp air.

Mornings in the kingdom of Faytrue carried a chill no matter the time of year. The continent itself was moderately far north so, though they were nestled south of the mountains, Riva couldn't recall a summer that did not require long sleeves, nor a winter that did not require constant hearth fires.

A few minutes passed with the sounds of chickens clucking and Benji crawling through the coop collecting eggs. His muffled grunts and squeals of glee with each egg found brought another laugh to Riva's lips.

"You know, there are the little doors." She pointed. "You don't have to go inside."

"It's more fun in here," Benji called back with a wicked little-boy-cackle. "I'm a chicken!"

She shook her head and wandered to the gate at the edge of the wide courtyard. A single guard stood on the other side. He offered a nod of acknowledgement before returning his gaze to the winding path that twisted along the far end of the grounds and toward the city.

As with every morning, Farmer Livingston trundled toward them with his usual delivery of milk, cheese, and fresh vegetables. There used to be many more, a whole pack of local merchants who would bring their goods to the castle for the king's table.

Those days were years ago, before the king had finally admitted to the country's financial trouble. Well, the country as a whole, but specifically the crown. Part of why Riva's sister had been so willing to marry a man nearly twice her age.

He was a nobleman. A rich nobleman and one from their country, which meant when she finally inherited the throne it would be a man from Faytrue as king. Not some stranger.

Not that Riva minded men from other lands...

Her thoughts drifted as she waited for Livingston to reach the gate. Memories of summer days laid out in a grassy field. A thin blanket beneath her head as she stared at the sky, glancing occasionally at the man beside her as he laughed and pointed to shapes in the clouds.

She missed his dark hair. The way his eyes glinted when he looked at her. The way he smiled when he said her name.

Riva gave her head a little shake. Her sister might be married, but they still had to wait for his older brother to wed before Charles could officially ask for her hand. And Derek, the crown prince of Cerulean, an island just south of the continent, was marrying for duty rather than love. Charles did not want to push him.

She understood. He was protecting his brother.

The ache of missing him still cramped her stomach.

Benji clattered out of the chicken coop behind her, sending up a cloud of dust, feathers, and squawking.

Riva chuckled and half turned to see if he was all right.

In that moment, with her gaze away from the gate, a loud crash rocked the air.

Riva flinched, her chest constricted, and golden light erupted from her hair.

Chapter Two

Impossible

Riva didn't have time to scream. Her breath caught in her throat as she concentrated every fiber of her being into pulling her errant power back into her braids. They were no longer tied into a knot at the base of her neck. Instead, they'd flown from their pins and whipped around her like cracking chains.

"Princess?" Benji's high, terrified voice cut through Riva's own panic.

She groaned with effort, putting her hands on either side of her head to smooth down the hair. She heaved tense breaths. With her eyes closed, she managed to pull the braids back down and calm the power within.

She stood still for a few seconds to ensure her odd, intense magic was restrained. She took half a step back upon opening her eyes. The guard's sword glinted a few inches from her chest. He looked at her with mistrust and fear. An expression she'd grown used to from much of the palace guard.

The others—servants, cooks, gardeners—they knew her. They'd shared meals together, done chores side by side, and spoke often. The guards, however, kept their distance on orders from the king.

It would be harder to strike her down if they thought of her as a friend.

"I'm sorry," Riva said with an exhale. She met the man's gaze with her chin raised. Dangerous power or no, she was still a princess. "The noise..."

She looked past the man and easily found the source of the crash which had startled her magic out of her. Farmer Livingston knelt beside his cart. A wheel had snapped, chunks of wood scattered across the ground along with many of the goods he was meant to deliver.

"Benji?" Riva called.

"Right here, Princess." The boy scurried to her side. His hair was a mess, cheeks flushed and eyes bright—with tears or excitement, she wasn't sure.

"Go let your mother know Livingston had an accident and will be a little late. I'll be back in a moment; I'm going to go help him."

Benji nodded, and the skip in his step suggested Riva hadn't scared him too much. A twinge of relief eased some of her nerves.

The guard had not lowered his weapon.

Riva met his gaze. She'd seen her own eyes in the mirror a few times after her "incidents," the term those close to her had deemed fit to use when describing her uncontrollable outbursts of magic. The gold lighting would still be flickering across her blue irises. It would last a few seconds more, maybe half a minute, before fading.

"I'd like to pass," she said, her voice steady.

The man took half a step back, bumping into the gate behind him. His sword hand trembled, and Riva wondered if he was new to the palace. She didn't recognize him.

"You're... you're not allowed outside the palace grounds," he stuttered.

Riva raised an eyebrow. A hot rush of embarrassment stirred through her empty stomach. None showed on her face.

"Very well." She gestured past the guard and his still-extended sword. "Go help the man yourself."

Finally, the guard looked toward the farmer. Riva's lips twitched into a deep scowl before she smoothed her expression. If there had been actual danger, this man would have wasted time and opportunity watching her instead of searching for a threat.

Then again... she swallowed down a lump in her throat, refusing to let it, or the burning in her eyes, turn into any sign of weakness.

"Highness..." The guard faltered again. There, at least, was the proper title.

"He requires assistance." Riva spoke softer this time.

The blade dipped, and she leaned in a fraction.

"I'm not a danger." There was pained tension in her tone. The words were true enough. At least right now.

"The noise startled me, that's all. If you won't let me pass, I ask that you go offer your help."

The guard hesitated then sheathed his weapon.

He swallowed, sweat glistening on his forehead, though the morning was still quite chilly. With a nod, almost a bow, he turned from her and went through the gate.

Riva strode across the courtyard to a niche between the chicken coop and the far stone wall. She slumped against the cold rock. Her shoulders shook, fingers trembling now that she was out of sight.

This had to stop. The frequency of incidents was increasing. New things sparked fear in her for no reason. It was as though her magic sensed something coming and was as on edge as an archer on watch during the Dark Season.

It often felt as though the golden light inside her was its own entity. One she had no control over.

Riva closed her eyes and breathed. The stale musk of hay, lifted by the distant salty sea air, brought relief to her nerves. The familiar scents grounded her. As did the stone beneath her boots, the wall to her back, and the clattering sounds coming from the open kitchen door.

After a moment, she wiped the tears from her cheeks. Her nimble fingers undid the frizzy braids on either side of her head, one at a time, draping the hair over her shoulder to keep it from dragging on the ground. With quick, practiced movements, she redid the braids. The usual strands of three no longer sufficed to keep her hair short enough to function. Instead, she worked with five locks, weaving them in and around each other until each side was done.

As fast as her fingers flew, it still took several minutes. They weren't her usual neat braids, but they'd do. And re-doing them hid the evidence of the incident itself, which was always noticeable in the frizzy mess her hair became every time.

By the time Riva walked back to the kitchen, the guard and Farmer Livingston were nearly to the wall with the small wagon. She contemplated going to hold the gate open for them, and then recalled the contempt in the guard's gaze and decided against it.

"Princess." Marian's voice carried a rare soothing edge as Riva stepped into the bustling kitchen. "Are you all right?"

"It would be easier if I could just cut the damn thing," Riva said in a furious whisper.

Marian put a hand on her arm. "I was there when yeh tried that as a child. I won't hear that screaming again, Princess. You leave those golden locks alone."

Riva gave a tight smile. She wiped her hands on her apron and gave half a nod. "I'm sorry I was gone for a bit. What can I help with?"

Benji perched on the counter near the stove, warming his hands rather dangerously a few inches from the kettle. He flashed a wide grin Riva's way. "Nothin'. The king wants you."

Marian's eyes rolled heavenward, and she gave a little shake of her head. "*His Majesty*," she said with a pointed glare at her son, "sent a missive for you a few minutes ago, Princess. He requires you in the throne room."

Riva bit the inside edge of her lower lip, a fresh thrill of anxiety clenching her gut. She dipped her head in a nod. "Thank you."

She straightened, brushed at her shirt with her hands, and made for the door.

"Princess," Marian murmured. "Your apron."

"Right." Riva untied her apron and hung it from a hook beside the door to the hallway.

Benji scooted from the counter, landing with a soft thud on the kitchen floor. "Good luck, Riva."

She chuckled and ruffled his hair. "Thanks."

"Benji," Marian scolded. "Don't be so informal."

The sounds of Benji's complaints of "It don't matter. She's my friend" followed Riva through the door and down the muted service hall.

Her father couldn't already know about the incident. It was impossible for the guard to have told him and helped the farmer at the same time.

It was also impossible for a girl to have magic hair that shot out golden sparks when something scared her. Impossible wasn't a word Riva appreciated.

The thought that her father had somehow heard of this most recent outburst was not a pleasant one.

Riva stopped before the door to the gilded palace halls and took another deep breath. There was no reason to think the king wanted her for anything awful. She opened the door and made her way to the throne room.

CHAPTER THREE

Not a Witch

The throne room of Faytrue's grand palace was as ornate and beautiful as any Riva had seen in her limited travels of the world. Trellises of vibrant flowers in subtle purples and blues accented the silver pillars lining the room. Silver decorated the windows as well, winding patterns of the metal threading across the glass.

Riva never looked as good in the family's colors as her elder sister. Larissa's dark hair and smooth, pale complexion went well with the silver gowns she often wore. On Riva, the color clashed with her hair as well as the smattering of freckles across her sun kissed skin.

Though not dressed for the occasion, she strode into the throne room with her head held high. Enough years of stacking books atop it had ingrained in her the ability to keep her neck rigid and her chin forward no matter the situation.

A handful of courtiers lined the grand room. Most she knew. A few she was friendly with. Half a dozen servants carried trays with small breakfast snacks. And two dozen of the royal guard lined the hall as they always did.

King Francis sat on his dazzling throne, atop a dais at the far end of the room. Crown Princess Larissa stood at his side, the position she took and kept when their mother had died so many years ago. Her husband was with the other courtiers. He had yet to earn a place on the dais.

Riva swallowed as she walked, overly aware of the eyes upon her. It was odd, to be called to her father like this. She always joined them for breakfast, which was normally another hour later. There was no need for her to be in the throne room—especially not dressed the way she was now.

Riva caught her sister's gaze as she neared, and a flash of worry went through her gut.

Larissa had been crying. She had a hand to her belly, a slight protrusion the only sign of the announcement the kingdom would soon share with the world. The baby was healthy; Riva knew this. Yet fear clutched her for the briefest of moments as she saw her sister's reddened eyes.

Riva exhaled through parted lips, about to ask if Larissa was all right, when her sister gave the briefest shake of her head and her gaze darted to the edge of the dais.

Riva followed her look.

A strange man stood not far from the king. In a kingdom their size, it was not unusual for Riva to be unfamiliar with the many lords who ventured to visit the king. But this man did not appear to be a lord.

His cloak was well worn, though made of quality material. He had the weathered face of an older man, jet black hair cut in a trim that had been stylish a few decades ago, and a silver locket dangled from his neck.

Riva returned her eyes to her sister, raising her eyebrows in a silent question before she bowed low and addressed their father.

"Your Majesty. You called?"

"I did." King Francis was never known for being a quiet man, and indeed his booming voice echoed through the mostly empty chamber. "Daughter, are you well?"

"Aye, father." Riva glanced at Larissa once again. The smile plastered on her face was one she often used in court, and it hid her nerves well. But Riva knew her.

Her sister pressed her lips into a thin line and looked away.

"Good, good." Francis looked over at the strange man. "We have news, my darling."

"News?" Riva said slowly, her gaze following her father's with unease growing in her stomach.

"Indeed. Good news. Good for the kingdom, good for the crown." He smiled, the skin around his eyes crinkling in a way Riva had loved as a child. Now, however, it brought no joy to her.

"I'm... happy to hear that." Riva's nerves finally got the best of her and, though her steady expression did not waver, her fingers began to twist the folds of her skirts.

"Father," Larissa said as Francis opened his mouth to speak again.

Riva's eyes widened a fraction before she returned them to neutral.

The king glared at his favorite child.

"I must reiterate my suggestion of a private conversation." Larissa, her glittering silver tiara resting gently upon her forehead, gave a slight deferential nod to her father. "I think... it would go over better without the eyes and ears of the court."

Fear clutched at Riva's chest. "What would, sister?"

Larissa's lips pressed together in that thin line again, and she said nothing.

"Father?" Riva took half a step toward him.

The king stood. "My darling, I'd like you to meet Lord Gadrel of the Hidden Hamlet."

The stranger stepped forward, put a hand to his chest, and bowed. "We're aiming for a better name," he said with a chuckle. "Given that we aren't hidden any longer, and that my lands are significantly more than a hamlet." A brief clench of his jaw accompanied his last few words.

Riva gave the obligatory smile upon meeting a lord and returned focus to her father.

"Sire?" she said, her voice low.

Francis waved a hand through the air. "Lord Gadrel is something of a wizard in his lands."

Riva took a full step backward. Her heartbeat quickened, and she noted her sister staring at the floor again.

"He hails from the border of Faytrue, in a segment of land not claimed by our kingdom, nor our neighbors. He's been waiting for one of us to recognize him as a sovereign state."

The training which had been so ingrained in Riva failed her at that moment. She'd been around enough royalty, enough politics, to know where this was going.

"Father..."

"Come now, Rivanissee."

She flinched at the use of her given name.

"Lord Gadrel has offered us a very generous trade deal. He knows of the magics that are forbidden here. Magics that might help your little problem."

At this, a low murmur went through the small crowd of onlookers.

Disbelief shattered within Riva's mind. The full reality of the situation slammed into her hard and fast.

She shook her head. "No."

"This is not a question, daughter," the king snapped. "You are a danger here. A slap in the face to the laws set down generations ago. Lord Gadrel has agreed to return with you to his lands, teach you to control your witchcraft, and wed you."

A rushing sound, like standing in a waterfall, overcame Riva's hearing. She staggered back. Around her, the courtiers took small steps toward the king, mouths open as though they might be objecting. Yet she heard none of it.

Hands gripped her upper arms, and she jerked her head wildly. Members of the royal guard held her tight. The wizard approached, the mask of kindness on his face given away by the wicked glint in his eye.

"I'm not a witch," Riva breathed.

The man nodded, casting a sympathetic look at the growing crowd around her.

King Francis raised a hand, and the commotion in the throne room ceased.

Riva's lip curled as the fear in her melted into anger. "I'm *not* a witch." She shouted it this time, calling up to her father with acid in her voice. "You cannot do this, Father."

What might have been sorrow, or at least regret, flickered briefly across his face. Then he steeled his resolve and waved his hand.

The guards began pulling her backward.

"I belong here," Riva called out, desperation sneaking into her tone. "I belong in Faytrue, *Father*." She glanced toward Larissa, silent tears now streaming down her pale cheeks. "Sister, you know I'm not. You know I'm not a witch. Don't. Please, *don't let him do this*!"

Her cries fell on deaf ears.

Sympathetic but powerless faces passed her as she was pulled from the throne room. Her shouts echoed through the halls of the palace as four guards dragged her to a coach waiting outside.

In desperation, she tried to summon the power within her. The magic that kept getting her in trouble. The magic that labeled her a witch.

Nothing happened.

CHAPTER FOUR

Not Quite Born for the Role

The oddity of being the only one in the palace who knew he had not been born the crown prince of Cerulean was always strange, occasionally problematic, and, in rare circumstances, detrimental. Charles adjusted the crown on his head for the dozenth time that day. He'd still not gotten used to the weight of it. His old one, which was now probably with his brother, was practically nothing in comparison.

"Your Highness."

Charles turned as a trusted friend and courtier caught up to him. They'd been the same age barely a month ago. Now he was older? Or was his brother younger? Had they switched or... the multitude of questions surrounding the magic done to move the crown to Charles's head had not lessened. If anything, it grew and continued to grow as each day passed.

"Yes, John?"

John, a strapping young lad who had attended classes with Charles and the other boys their age, was third born in his family and wore the lack of title well. Even if Charles was older now, it would only be a bit more than a year. Hardly any difference.

At least, that's what Charles told himself when the confusing thoughts of magic muddled his mind at night, stopping him from getting enough sleep for his duties. Duties which were new to him but which everyone else expected him to already know and understand.

John grinned up at Charles, his deep auburn skin almost golden in the early morning light. "The king requests your presence in the map room."

Yet another oddity. The use of the word request. As the second son in the royal family, Charles had spent his life hearing orders and commands. As crown prince, his father treated him with a different level of respect.

Charles nodded. "Thank you. I'll join him there shortly. Has he spent time with the girls today?"

John's expression warmed. "He ate with the little ones. They're in lessons now, but I did overhear a promise to teach Princess Tilly the intricacies of saddling a horse later this afternoon."

Comforting arms of satisfaction wrapped around Charles.

There were many good things about the magic his brother had unleashed when he'd broken the deal with the sea witch. Derek was free, no longer bound to marry a woman he barely knew and didn't love. No longer locked safely within the confines of Lagonia, the glistening capital city that held the royal palace.

Charles now carried the duty of finding a bride. Fortunately, the freedom of his previous life had allowed him the opportunity to find such a woman. Riva of Faytrue. As in love with him as he was with her and, until now, willing to wait to marry until Charles's beloved brother was ready.

That particular obstacle was no longer an issue. And, as Charles already had the blessing of his father, the only thing holding them up was how long it took for the messenger to deliver his proposal to Riva's father. If the weather had been kind, Charles could expect a response within a few days.

Beyond the happiness of his brother, himself, and his future bride, Charles had also instituted a few changes that Derek—as wonderful and kind as he was—knew not to initiate.

The shadow Derek had cast over the rest of the children in their family had been purely accidental and no fault of his own. That fact did not diminish the pain felt by the little ones at their father's utter lack of attention.

Charles still was not used to the king looking directly at him on such a regular basis, speaking to him like an equal—or something close to it—and asking his opinion on matters not just of state, but personal as well.

So, when the first week of being crown prince had settled in and Charles had begun to adjust to his new/old position, he'd taken his father aside for a serious conversation that would not have been possible without the witch's spell.

The middle siblings—boy and girl twins—who were teenagers and uninterested in their father's sudden affection, would eventually benefit from the weekly family dinners Charles had put in place. But the change in the three youngest princesses was already visible. The girls' time with their father brought out confidence, curiosity, and a level of respect for the kingdom itself, which had been somewhat lacking due to both their ages and what had felt like near invisibility.

"Highness?"

Charles blinked, surprised to find himself and John already standing at the doors to the map room.

"Sorry, John. In my own head again." He chuckled. "Being crown prince is... a bit much at times."

"A role you were born for, Charles."

Charles snorted, earning a politely brief look of incredulity from his friend.

"Thank you," Charles said, stifling his laughter. "And thank you for coming to get me."

John nodded, dipping into a bow, then straightened and flashed his wide grin. "If you have time later, a race?"

"I'm sure I can fit in an hour to make a fool of you."

Both men chuckled and, with the promise of meeting at the stable in the afternoon, went their separate ways.

The map room, also known as the war room when the occasion called for it, was a massive thing. Second only to the grand throne room, it stretched well over twenty feet high and was lined with rows and rows of bookshelves. The far wall was covered almost entirely in maps. The world map was replaced every few years, new lines and borders drawn as less peaceful kingdoms and empires battled over every disagreement. Around it were more detailed depictions of different countries, secret entrances to towering mountains, routes through treacherous oceans, and paths of individuals under the crown's watchful eye.

Derek was one of those little blue lines.

Charles had been startled to know his father had kept tabs on *him* during each of his adventures away from Lagonia. The spymasters of Cerulean were second to none—something Charles had not been privy to until he became crown prince.

"Father," Charles called as he strode into the wide space. Comfortable armchairs clustered near the bookshelves, but the king was nearly always found at the massive center table. He had a desk only a few yards away. Charles had yet to see him sit at it.

"Ahh, my boy." King Victor the Magnanimous—who preferred that title to his full and very long name—offered a wide smile to his son as Charles approached.

Derek had gotten his features from the queen. His pale skin, blonde hair, and blue eyes were passed down nearly entirely from their mother. Charles, on the other hand, had inherited his father's looks.

The king had been a handsome young man, unless the portrait artisans were skilled liars, and was somehow becoming more distinguished with age. His dark hair had only recently shown signs of greying. The salt and pepper around his ears matched his mustache and beard: both healthy, thick, and well groomed. His eyes, as dark as the queen's had been light, glistened with intelligence and insight. Even his shoulders, which might have been stooped from age, loss, and the weight of the throne, were straight and strong.

Victor clapped an arm around Charles and led him to the table. "I've been going over who to invite to the wedding. There are a number of merchants we may gain favor with if they're included."

Charles let out a good-natured laugh. "Father, I have yet to hear back from Princess Riva. Perhaps we wait until her family has accepted my proposal before we send out invitations."

The king waved a hand, glistening with rings, through the air. "Of course we will wait to complete the list until advisors from Faytrue are able to confirm their guests. But you've told me enough about the girl, Charles, that I'm certain she is as taken with you as you are with her."

Charles felt his cheeks going red and busied himself with fiddling through the stack of papers on the table.

"Any important affairs of the kingdom I should know about?"

Victor laughed, a deep booming sound that echoed through the room. "All right. I understand not wanting to discuss the matter with your father. I've been there myself. When your mother and I were preparing for our wedding day, both my parents felt the need to have their noses in the affair."

Charles's eyes widened, and he huffed out a chuckle of disbelief. "And you let them?"

"Let them? Son, this was before I became king. Things were quite different back then. Your mother encouraged you, Derek, and your siblings to speak to us with honesty and blatant truths. That was not the way when I was young."

Charles nodded. He was fully aware of the changes his progressive mother had made as queen. She had ruffled many feathers at court before people realized how beneficial her actions were to the country at large.

The king and the crown prince circled the massive table, taking their time with different sets of important documents. Victor's method of teaching was something Charles wasn't used to, and he didn't have the benefit of the years of training that everyone thought he did.

Still, he'd always been quick on his feet and knew how to improvise. His questions sounded more like confirmations than inquiries. It didn't take more than a few hours for the two of them to get through the majority of the business for the day.

"I'm off to the stables," Charles said when his father finally suggested they excuse themselves for a reprieve. "Racing with John."

The king chuckled. "Be safe, my boy. And make sure you win."

Charles nodded with a grin and went to find his friend.

John wasn't at the stables when Charles arrived.

He spent some time preparing his horse and chatting with the stable boy. Just as he was beginning to worry, John came into view, hurrying toward them from the direction of the palace gates.

He carried a slip of parchment in his hands.

Charles jogged down the gravel path to meet him, curiosity and mild concern in the furrow of his brow. "John, everything all right?"

"I'm not sure, Highness." John handed over the note. "The messenger carrying this seemed... ill at ease."

Charles took the paper, heart leaping to his throat as he recognized the royal seal of Faytrue. He ripped it open, giddiness dancing in his stomach.

A chill took his body at the formality with which his name was written. The cold seeped through him as he read; tears of heartbreak, then anger burned in his eyes.

He reached the end of the letter, folded the paper, and turned to John.

"I don't care how you do it: raven, messenger, or some back-alley channel. But get Derek here."

"Highness?" Apprehension filled John's voice. "Is everything all right?"

"No." Charles met John's eye, grinding his teeth to keep from shouting. "Get my brother here. Now."

CHAPTER FIVE

Greggory the Mouse

"Are you entirely certain this is the way?" Derek's hoarse whisper carried down the dark tunnel in which he crouched.

Ahead of him, dressed in bracers, a black tunic, black gloves, and a black scarf to hold her hair in place, Symphonia the sea witch turned a set of glaring, glinting eyes on him.

"If I wasn't certain, we wouldn't be going this way."

Derek raised an eyebrow. After a month traveling together, he knew that statement was not entirely true.

Sym huffed, her breath a fog on the chilly air. "The mouse said it was this way."

Derek let out a silent chuckle as his friend turned and continued her stooped trudge through the tunnel. It was handy, traveling with a companion who was able to cast spells, talk to animals, and generally get him out of the constant trouble he often found himself in.

Life as a crown prince hadn't entirely prepared him for a sudden thrust into the real world. As evidenced by his utter lack of success during the first attempt at this current venture.

They were in a drainage tunnel, designed to withstand the heavy storms found in the northern mountains of Cerulean. With any luck, and if the mouse had been telling the truth, they were close to Baron Stalk's kitchen court-yard. The castle itself was well guarded, especially after the Baron's youngest son had angered another powerful fam-ily in the area. But drainage pipes were often overlooked.

"There's the light," Sym muttered, a bit of a grumble in her tone.

"Excellent." Derek ignored her grumpiness and scooched forward. "Nearly dawn. We should hurry."

A bit of oil on the hinges to the grate, some light grunt-ing as Derek pushed with all his strength, and the two of them were able to tumble silently onto the cobble-stone. The icy bite of pre-sunrise in the mountains stung at Derek's fingers and ears. He glanced over at Sym, who was used to the chill of the ocean but not the brittle, dry air of the mountains.

She shivered, the cracks in her coppery skin growing white with frost.

A full month into traveling together every day, sharing a room at each inn, and trading cooking duties, and he'd yet to gain the courage to ask about the black breaks in her skin. They shifted, changing with her use of magic. Sometimes he worried the ones around her jaw would reach her lips and crack her face in two. Other times they shrank so much he almost didn't see them.

"Inside," Derek said with a jerk of his head.

They hurried to the door to the kitchen. It would soon be bustling with breakfast preparation, but for now there were few people up and about. One of the reasons to trek to a drainage pipe, climb in, and crawl their way to the castle before the horizon gained any color from the approaching sun.

Their dark clothes helped them blend into the stone used to construct Baron Stalk's castle. Small when compared to the glittering palace Derek had grown up in, Stalks' home was still a multi-level maze.

The man had a dozen children, many of whom lived in different wings with their families. The grand hall, which Derek had seen firsthand when he'd given diplomacy a try the day before, was almost as large as the grand throne room in Lagonia. It was, however, not nearly as warm.

Derek took a right turn, then paused as something squeaked at his feet.

"Greggory! It's not safe for you here. You were supposed to wait by the tunnel."

The absurdity of Sym's soft scolding nearly made Derek burst into a fit of laughter.

She bent, and a small grey mouse scurried into her out-stretched palm. The little thing put a paw to its whiskers, twirling the ends as it carried on squeaking.

Derek glanced down either stretch of the hallway, disliking the lack of a hiding place.

"Ohh, I see. Yes, thank you, Greggory." Sym leaned in toward Derek. "We need to go that way." She pointed the opposite direction he'd been about to go.

"No," he whispered back. "The grand hall is that way. I'm sure of it."

"Yes, prince," she sighed with a tone of incredulity he'd almost gotten used to. "But the treasure room is, in fact, *that* way."

The mouse, standing on two legs in Sym's palm, pointed a paw. Derek leaned around her to look down the long, windowless hallway.

He addressed the mouse. "You're certain they've moved the goose? Because it was in the hall yesterday."

The mouse put a paw to its chest and gave a solemn nod.

Derek pressed his fingers to the bridge of his nose. He'd thought being given a tail, spending three days searching the ocean for his fiancé, and then trading his title as crown prince with his little brother was strange. Now he was talking to a mouse.

"Very well," he muttered. "We're running short on time. Let's hurry."

Derek understood immediately why the Stalk family had moved the golden feathered farm animal to the treasure room. It was a windowless space, walled with massive paintings in ornate frames. Shelves of gold, silver, jewels, and more took up a third of the room. Standing vases, candle sticks, even a miniature replica of a carriage accented with pearls, filled in much of the rest.

The lock had been beyond Derek's ability to pick, but the mouse—who seemed not to like the owners of the castle he lived in—brought them a key.

They moved slowly through the dark interior. Sym brought forth a mote of light, letting it hover a few feet above them in the center of the room. She took careful steps, not touching anything but eyeing each artifact with heavy interest.

Their objective was easily found. A stack of shelves had been shunted aside to make room for the massive cage pressed in the corner. In it, huddled with her feathers stuck up in fear, was a vibrant white goose streaked through with golden accents.

"Oh my," Derek muttered.

He took a step, but Sym's hand latched around his arm, locking him in place.

"Be careful, Derek." Her tone made him hesitate.

He met her dark gaze. "What's wrong?"

"There are... things here." She winced, her head twisting to the side. She blinked rapidly and tapped her nails against her cheek.

The little black lines, like cracks in porcelain, grew ever so slightly.

Derek's hand went to the hilt on his belt. "What kind of things?"

There was a pause, then Sym shook her head, locks of braided and twisted black hair dangling this way and that. "Nothing that will attack us. But there is heavy magic here. The kind your kingdom has been unfamiliar with for many generations."

Derek frowned. It wasn't her words that sent unease through his stomach—though the idea of a prickly northern baron having access to magic the capital didn't was not ideal. It was the way she spoke. Her voice took on a distant, echoey sound.

He was reminded of their first meeting. In a dark ocean cave, green light casting shadows across every wrinkled surface, and Sym, dressed in an old sail and speaking in riddles. And alone.

She'd been so alone.

He hadn't realized it when they first started their journey north. He'd thought her odd mannerisms and rhythmic words were because she was a witch, over a hundred years old and capable of magics that changed the course of a full bloodline and kingdom.

It turned out she was entirely unused to being around people.

"Sym?" Derek said, concerned.

"These are..." She walked along one of the rows, her hand hovering over the artifacts. She paused at a glistening pair of glass slippers. "These are very old, Derek. These should not be here."

Derek took a step toward her, touching her arm. "I hear you, Sym. We won't let them stay. But right now..."

"Of course." Sym shook her head. Focus returned to her eyes as she pulled her hand away. She turned to the goose in the corner of the room. "We have another job to do."

A smile crooked the edge of Derek's lips. "How, exactly, are we getting a giant bird out of the castle without being seen?"

Sym rubbed her hands together as the little mouse, who was still with them, scurried up her sleeve and stood at her shoulder. It squeaked.

"Exactly," Sym said with a grin.

Derek opened his mouth, uttered a slightly pained sound, and said, "You know I can't understand the mouse, right?"

She chuckled, patted the little rodent on its head, and strode to the goose. "Size is tricky." She walked around the side of the cage, tilting her head as she surveyed the creature inside. "But you're mostly fluff, aren't you?"

Derek followed her, raising an eyebrow as she murmured to herself and gently prodded the goose's feathers.

"All right. Take a step back," she said to Derek. "Just in case this goes the wrong way."

"The wrong way?" he asked, taking several steps back rather than one.

"This thing is either going to get small enough for us to sneak it out, or it will get bigger."

Derek's eyes widened. He opened his mouth to tell her to wait.

But she raised her hands and began chanting.

CHAPTER SIX

Beans

Derek released a whooping laugh. He urged his horse onward, galloping at breakneck speed over the rolling hills. Dew covered grass bent beneath the beast's hooves.

Ahead of him, Sym cackled as well, her horse moving faster than should have been possible. The thing still reeked of saltwater and fish.

Derek pulled gently on the reins as they rounded a tall stack of stones. They were well out of sight of Baron Stalk's castle. A good mile of heavily textured land between them and anyone who might wake now that the sun had risen and discover a missing treasured possession.

He glanced at the little wicker cage securely strapped to the back of his saddle. In it, barely bigger than the mouse who had hitched a ride with Sym, was the golden goose.

"How long, exactly," Derek inhaled, winded from the adrenaline and giddiness, "will this spell last?"

"Good question." Sym's lips parted in a wicked grin. "We should hurry."

He huffed an incredulous sigh, wheeled his horse, and kicked into a steady trot. The giant's farm was a couple hours away, and Derek didn't fancy his horse being squished by a massive goose halfway there.

He admired the landscape as they went. The north continued to hit him with bursts of awe. Traveling the old but well-maintained roads with a royal guard didn't come close to *this*. The freedom of riding cross country with nothing and no one between him and the next adventure.

A brief flicker of doubt interrupted his easy smile. Charles had taken his place in the palace. Taken on the duties and responsibilities that Derek had been born to. And, though his brother had reassured him it was all right, ideal even, there was a part of Derek that would never stop worrying about the burden he'd placed on one of the people he loved most in the world.

He wondered for a moment when he'd hear from the new crown prince. There was to be a wedding soon. At least that was what Charles had suggested when Derek had left.

He and Sym had yet to receive word of a date to be back in Lagonia. Perhaps they'd start heading that way again after they dropped off the goose.

They arrived at the farm just as Derek's stomach began its midday grumbling. Massive wooden pillars towered on either side of a gate that stretched twice as tall as Derek and three times the length of his horse. To him, it looked like a palace of its own. To the giant family who lived there it was a simple barrier marking their property.

Derek shook his head as they trotted through the open gate. Charles had spoken of giants a few times. Derek always thought he was exaggerating.

"Prince Derek, my good man."

Derek turned his flinch into a cough before he dismounted and grinned up at the massive man sitting a few yards away.

Dorsitch Goatsherd looked very similar to a regular man. Except for the fact that he was about twenty-four feet tall. His long sandy colored hair was braided into two chunks, almost identical to the way he styled his beard. Dorsitch's voice was low and slow. The vibration from his baritone almost seemed to chatter Derek's teeth.

"Mister Goatsherd." Derek tied his horse off on the bottom rung of a nearby ladder and turned to his recently made friend. "How was your night?"

Dorsitch chuckled, leaning back on the edge of his finely finished wooden porch. The entirety of his house was nearly a quarter the size of the palace in Lagonia. It likely started as a simple cottage—for a giant. But with a growing family, Dorsitch had needed to add on rooms here and there.

Rooms the size of stables.

"T'was a fine evening. Though the missus was a mite worried when she noticed our small-folk friends were not in their beds when the sun rose."

"Ahh yes," Sym said as she strode over to the giant's knee. "We might have left a note, Derek."

Derek nodded, grinning at her chagrining tone. "I'm sorry to have worried her."

"All for good reason, I hope?" Dorsitch raised a bushy eyebrow, a smile peeking from the corners of his mustache.

"I hope so as well," Derek said. He unbuckled the wicker basket holding the golden bird and carried it to the waiting giant. "I think we found something that belongs to you."

"*Found*, is it?" He leaned down, inspecting the basket as Derek held it up. **"I hope that's not my bird, Highness. She'd have to lay a dozen eggs for me to get one bite."**

Derek barked out a laugh, opened the cage, and set it on the ground. "Sym?"

The witch let out a little cackle and, with impressive speed, chanted once again.

It took barely a few seconds for the goose to begin growing. She flapped her wings a few times, looked nervously at the wicker on either side of her, and darted out the open door. By the time she'd settled down, she was back to her regular—massive—size.

"That's more like it," the giant chuckled. He cast a worried glance down at Derek. **"You didn't stir up any trouble with the Baron, did you?"**

Derek waved a lazy hand through the air. "No. It didn't take much to figure out Jack hadn't told his father where he'd caught the goose. I doubt the Baron is fool enough to actually pick a fight with you, Goatsherd."

The giant laughed again, shaking the ground beneath them all as he stamped a soft leather-clad shoe into the dirt.

"That boy is trouble," Dorsitch said when his laughter faded. **"Wanted to buy some big animals."** He gestured a hand toward the pasture of oversized beasts around the far side of the house. **"But all he offered for them were beans. Because I am a giant, because I talk slower than you little-folk, he took me for a fool. Then, when I turn down his ridiculous offer, he steals from me."** Dorsitch shook his head, disgust lined into the creases of his weathered skin. **"Despicable."**

"Indeed." Sym nodded vigorously. "It is always insulting to be so underestimated."

Derek glanced at her, wondering if there was a deeper meaning behind her words. But she kept her gaze on the giant.

Not long after they'd gotten water for the horses and Sym introduced Dorsitch to Greggory, with Derek politely reminding her that the giant couldn't understand mice any better than he could, their host invited them to a midday meal.

The food was delicious, the portions massive, and the cutlery hilariously difficult to use. Dorsitch's youngest child, four years old and as big as Derek, tried desperately to teach the prince how to use the fork until his mother pointed out it was a matter of gripping it more than lack of education.

The table rumbled with laughter. They ate their fill, and then Derek and Sym began the discussion of where to go next.

"You might not have to make the choice," Dorsitch said from the window above the kitchen counter.

Derek followed his gaze. A raven, jet black with a cord of gold around its neck, flew toward the house.

"We don't know anyone who sends a raven," the giant continued. He looked at Derek. **"That's for you."**

CHAPTER SEVEN

Small Victories

Riva gave up her protests once the carriage had trundled across the wide stone bridge separating the capital of Faytrue from the expanse of farmlands to the northeast. She leaned against the door, breathing heavily and wishing she'd never left the damn kitchen.

Her favorite apron was still there, hung on a hook by the door. How long would Marian leave it before she tossed it away or gave it to a new servant hired to take the place of the princess?

An ache spread through her chest with her next breath. She clenched a hand at her side, fighting back the tears that wanted to fall.

There were words she should have said to her father. Arguments she didn't have time for but couldn't help being mad for not raising. A trade deal would mean little if she wasn't there to talk with their contacts in the lumber and fishing industries. The finances had just begun steadying, with *her* careful eye on the royal purse.

Then there was Charles. Gods, why hadn't she mentioned Charles? For the same reason her father didn't know about him in the first place—because the rumors and suspicions that would be raised if she had told him about the prince would likely have ruined her. She and the man she loved hadn't met in any official capacity. They'd been in love before either of them realized the other was royalty.

Larissa knew. She knew Riva was practically engaged. They'd talked about it a handful of times. Larissa's sisterly concern had aggravated Riva. But now she hoped Larissa had kept the threatening promise to keep tabs on Prince Charles. Her worry had been him hurting Riva, but maybe she could send word.

Maybe he'd come for her.

Maybe he'd never know what happened. Would, perhaps, think she went willingly. Think she abandoned him to marry this...

Riva turned her attention to the man sitting across from her. He lazed on the thick seat, one arm on his lap and the other resting on the top of the back cushion. Upon closer inspection, Riva was certain he was at least in his forties. Though, as a wizard it was possible he was much older.

Her knowledge of magic and how it aged a person was limited. Such things had been outlawed in Faytrue generations ago, part of why the royal family had worked so hard to keep her odd power a secret.

"How did you find out about me?"

Lord Gadrel cast a mild gaze upon her. "What do you mean?"

She shifted, glaring at him. "You came to the palace for a reason, Lord Gadrel. I find it hard to believe that it would start with a simple trade and end with an engagement."

He raised and dropped a shoulder, the ease in him sending shards of anger through Riva. "Such things are not unheard of."

"That's not a denial."

"No." The corner of his mouth twitched up, a crooked smile adding to his admittedly handsome features. He wasn't ugly by any means, not with his thick hair and broad frame.

The only thing he stirred in Riva was suspicion.

"So you knew of me and my magic before coming to the palace."

Gadrel nodded. "I'd heard rumors of a witch—"

"I'm not a witch," Riva snapped. The bite in her words came not only from the situation, but the implication that came with being called such a thing. Other kingdoms might be more lax, but in Faytrue the word came with a death sentence.

He sneered. "If you're not a witch, then you're cursed. Either way is not ideal in the backwards land you call home."

Riva clenched her jaw to keep from responding. A shot of pain came with the truth of his words. She turned away from him, no longer interested in how he came to find her or anything else he might say. Fields of golden wheat breezed by as they trundled along. Panic grew, wilted, and crumbled into anger within Riva the further they went.

Gadrel responded to her silence in kind.

They didn't speak again until the carriage pulled to a stop. The day had passed, and Riva's stomach growled with hunger. Orange tinted the sky, and hope glinted in her heart.

They were far from the palace now. Far from the guards. She'd find an opportunity to slip from Gadrel's clutches. Magic or not, he wouldn't be able to keep her.

That thought wavered as Gadrel stepped from the carriage. She followed and was struck with shock.

What she'd assumed was a horse drawn carriage, driven by a servant or guard of some sort, was only a carriage. Nothing pulled it. No one drove. The seat was empty, no harnesses for beasts of any kind.

She wheeled, staring as Lord Gadrel let out a chuckle.

"Wizard," he said, spreading his arms in a mocking bow.

Riva swallowed, scowling, and tried to keep a mask over the alarm that came with knowing he was this powerful.

"Wizard." He straightened. "And decent fiancé. I've found us a lovely place for the night."

Riva couldn't deny the inn behind him was lovely. Ivy crawled across stone walls on the first floor. The second was patterned with wood panels, wide windows closed for the night glowed with a soft warm light.

"I won't be staying the night with you, Lord Gadrel." The trembling in her fingers didn't reach her voice. Small victories, she supposed, as the wizard cocked his head.

"Of course not."

Her brows pinched together, suspicious confusion sending a rush of cold through her veins.

Gadrel's lips curled into a smile that didn't meet his eyes. "We aren't married yet, Princess. I'm a wizard, not a barbarian. And I won't have anything risk the legitimacy of our nuptials."

A brief flash of relief was struck down by the reminder of a coming marriage.

No. Not a coming marriage, because they would never get that far. She'd be gone by morning. She had no money on her person, nothing to sell, but she'd make for the coast. Surely a ship would take her to Cerulean in exchange for work. She didn't have a princess's hands, after all. They'd see her dedication in the calluses on her palms and the strength of her fingers.

"Don't dawdle," Gadrel called from the door to the inn. "I'm hungry."

Riva glared but followed him. Her stomach also clamored for food, and there was no point in running before he fell asleep. A man with magic enough to move a carriage to the border of the country with no horse absolutely had the ability to stop her in her tracks.

And, without the ability to rely on *her* power to help, the smart thing was to wait.

CHAPTER EIGHT

Heard

The cold helplessness of her current situation thawed with a sturdy bowl of stew and a chunk of fresh bread. The inn, and the family who ran it, was lovely. Riva chatted with the wife, a woman named Britta who gave her an extra portion of the rice pudding they had for dessert.

Riva didn't miss the look that passed between the innkeeper and his wife as Lord Gadrel asked for two rooms. It matched her own relief.

As evening faded and darkness fell, Riva found herself settled by the dining room fire. She warmed her feet before the steady glowing blaze. Her fingers worked across her scalp, massaging away the ache that came from carrying her hair all day.

The mass of it was still bundled at the base of her neck and had begun to make her skin itch. She usually had it down by now. Hanging from a hook near her bed as she read or kept up her journal before falling asleep.

Footsteps drew her gaze from the fire. She turned, hands folding in her lap at the sight of Lord Gadrel. He moved toward her and sat on a neighboring bench. She watched as he stared at the fire for a long moment before finally looking at her.

"I believe we started off in a rather unfortunate way."

Riva raised an eyebrow. Only growing up with her father's curt lack of humor kept her from snapping a sarcastic remark about kidnapping. "That's true. Though I'm not sure what a fortunate way would be, given the circumstance."

Gadrel sighed. He glanced behind them where a few patrons were finishing their meals. Britta, though too far away to hear their conversation, watched them with wary, guarded eyes.

"I wish it were different," Gadrel said. He reached into his long cloak, digging longer than should have been necessary, and pulled out a medium-sized black box with a silver design painted on the top. "I have this for you."

Riva's brow furrowed. She reached for it with tentative hands. "What is it?"

He gave a one-sided shrug. "A token. And hopefully a useful one, given..." He looked uncomfortable for a moment, then gestured to her hair.

Riva set the box on her lap and flipped the small latch. She opened it slowly, unsure what to expect, and blinked in surprise.

A set of hair cuffs, similar in style to a pair she had back home, rested on a bed of velvet. They were silver, inlaid with floral designs, and each larger than any others she'd seen before.

It would take a while, but with them she could loop her hair enough to let it hang somewhat free. The golden locks would still reach past her waist, but it would give her neck a break from the weight of the massive bun.

"I..." Her stomach clenched as anger fought propriety. "Thank you," she said softly.

Gadrel rose with a tired groan. "I hope we can start fresh in the morning." He waited, watching her for acknowledgement.

Riva was silent but gave a small nod. It seemed to be enough as he turned and headed up the stairs of the inn.

Riva took the cuffs, C-shaped with little silver clasps to help hold her hair in place, and examined them in the glint of the firelight. They were stunning.

She waited until most of the inn had retired for the night. Until the fire was burning low. Until Britta locked the door and secured it with a thick beam of wood.

Then Riva let down her hair.

She parted it down the middle, and then started at the ends, brushing her fingers through the silky strands until she was left with smooth flowing locks.

She took one of the silver cuffs and positioned it a few inches below her ear. With practiced movements, she began the arduous process of looping her hair again and again, finally securing it with the clasp.

"Would you like me to do the other?"

Riva jerked, her heart racing. She took a breath as Britta eased onto the seat beside her.

"Didn't mean to scare you, dear." The older woman's gaze followed the flow of Riva's remaining loose hair all the way to the puddle of it at her feet. "That's quite a lot of hair."

Riva nodded with a bitter smile. "It is."

"Would you like me to do the other side? I imagine your hands are tired," Britta said with a chuckle.

Riva let out a small laugh in return. "Always. It's a lot to maintain."

"Here." Britta moved closer, gesturing for Riva to turn.

The princess obeyed, handing over the other cuff.

The feeling of a kind set of hands on her hair, a cause of such strife in her life, was calming. Riva relaxed, the heartbreak of the day fading into the distance as she watched the embers dance in the hearth.

"Are you trying to keep it a secret?" Britta asked, her voice soft.

Riva turned her head just enough to meet the woman's eyes, her brow lightly furrowed in curiosity.

"We know who you are, your Highness."

Riva exhaled a puff of air. Her eyes burned. "It's no secret, though I've never felt the need to shout about it."

Britta nodded, her fingers making quick work of Riva's hair. "I wasn't sure, traveling with no escort and a man not native to Faytrue... I didn't want to make a fuss of it, if you were runnin' from something."

Riva rubbed her nose with the back of her hand and brushed away a tear. "I'm not running." She inhaled. "Not yet."

Britta paused for a brief second, seeming to mull over her words. When her hands picked up their work, she leaned closer to Riva. "There is much talk in the kingdom of late. Defaults on payments from the crown. Even after the royal wedding."

Riva gritted her teeth. Larissa's marriage was meant to fix much of that, but such things would take time. "Indeed, Faytrue has many debts."

"The most recent rumor, Highness, came to me after you arrived this evening. A messenger, delivering his usual news as well as gossip from the capital."

Riva closed her eyes; the ache in her heart grew as Britta spoke. The muddled mess that had been her day, and was now her life, tightened the muscles in her back. Her voice was soft, tired. "What have you heard?"

"The man you travel with, he is a wizard?"

Riva nodded.

"From the outlands? The Hidden Hamlet on the other side of the border?"

She nodded again.

"And..." Britta's voice went tight. A well worked hand rested on Riva's shoulder. "The king, he made a deal?"

"A trade," Riva whispered.

Without another word, Britta pulled Riva to her. The princess fell into the innkeeper's arms. Her forehead pressed to the woman's shoulder, tears hidden in her clothes.

Full minutes passed as Riva took every inch of comfort Britta offered and held it to her heart. The hurt of her situation thudded in the background of each heartbeat. But beyond marriage, betrayal, and the sting of being no more than an object in her father's eyes, lay the ache of missing the people back at the palace.

Marian, Benji, the maids, servants, governesses, and even a few courtiers, all left behind without so much as a goodbye. The plans Riva had made, betterments for her country built on the foundation she'd learned of from Charles, ideas she'd snuck to Larissa that they might be implemented when she took the throne... what would become of them now? What would become of her friends without her royal blood between them and the more vicious members of the ruling class?

"He's not gone to sleep yet," Britta whispered, grounding Riva from her thoughts and back to the little inn. "The light is on in his room. I will tell you when it goes out."

Riva pulled away, pressing palms to her eyes as more tears threatened to fall. "I don't want you involved. If someone found out you helped me—"

"I have friends, Highness," Britta broke across her words with tears of her own choked in her voice. "Women who work in the palace, men who serve the various lords of our lands." Her dark eyes met Riva's and held them. Her lips trembled. "I know what you've done for the people of this kingdom. Time and again, the sacrifices you've made to keep the regular folk safe. To get justice for us when someone who has all the power abuses it. Your voice is heard through Faytrue. By us."

Words abandoned Riva. Thoughts and emotions roiled as she recalled a handful of the most recent situations Britta spoke of. She had no idea anyone had noticed. No idea anyone had been cataloging the times she'd stepped in, either before the court or behind it, to be a voice for the people born to lower stations.

"I didn't..."

"The door will be unlocked," Britta murmured. She put a hand to Riva's cheek. "Faytrue will be lesser without you. But you deserve your own life."

She stood, and the lack of touch left Riva feeling cold. "I will knock once when the light goes out."

Riva nodded and stood as well. She inhaled through barely parted lips, still reeling from their conversation. "Thank you."

Britta smiled. "Off to bed, Highness."

Chapter Nine

Lost Names

Charles stood on the walkway of the great stone palace wall, staring out into the city streets of Lagonia. Mid-afternoon sun beat down on him, its temperature mild so close to the ocean. His fingers moved restlessly, flipping a large gold coin around and around, over and over while he waited for sight of the riders he knew would be coming soon.

His missive had reached Derek. And his brother had not hesitated. A return message, sent by magic, had blasted into Charles's ear in the middle of dinner. He'd leapt a foot, spilled a large goblet of wine, and scared his sisters. But once all was cleaned and a brief explanation was given to his father, they'd mostly understood.

Mostly, because when Charles had said he planned to go with Derek to rescue the woman he loved, his father forbade it.

There was no telling the truth about the sea witch traveling with Derek. So, for the purposes of explaining, she was someone with magic Derek had found along the way to the giants.

Charles's lip twitched into the briefest of grins. He wondered how his brother had fared in the north. Even their father didn't have a full grasp of the mountainous region of their island country. The giants and magics there were something Charles would not overlook when he became king.

He glanced to the guards on either side of him, and the grin melted away. Rumbling frustration coursed through his bones. They were doing their jobs, these men-at-arms who had been tailing him since he'd mentioned Riva's fate to his father. The idea of the crown prince running off to rescue the love of his life in a foreign land was not one the king could fathom.

Never mind the fact that it had already happened when Derek was still the crown prince. His entire escapade had led to this. Led to Charles being stuck behind the palace walls with glorified nursemaids keeping him home.

He shook his head to rid it of such thoughts. None of this was his brother's fault, and it especially wasn't the fault of the men charged with his protection. Besides, he knew his brother. Once Derek and Sym arrived, there was little that would be able to stop the three of them from making straight for the bastard who'd taken Riva.

"Highness," one of the guards said, lifting a gloved hand to point down the main boulevard that led through the city to the palace gates.

Charles leaned forward, excitement flushing his cheeks at the sight of two horses moving as quickly as was safe on such busy streets. Derek's dark mount kicked up a fair amount of dust behind it. The witch's seemed to leave a faint trail of water.

Charles shook his head as the two rode through the gate and then hurried down the courtyard to meet them.

While worry still wriggled like snakes in his stomach, any shred of frustration with his brother disintegrated when he saw Derek's face.

He couldn't recall, even thinking back to when their mother was alive, a time when Derek had looked happier. More at peace.

Even with the concern that flashed across his brother's face as he dismounted, passed the reins to a waiting stable-boy, and rushed to Charles's side. Even as Derek broke into a hurried series of questions about Riva, the letter, the plan, there was a freedom in his eyes that filled Charles's heart with happiness.

"Calm yourself, brother," Charles said, clapping a hand onto Derek's shoulder. "You've ridden a long way. Let's get you some food. We can discuss on the way."

"Might I see that letter?" The sea witch strode up to them. Behind her, a stable boy clutched the dripping reins of a horse that smelled suspiciously of salt water.

"Of course." Charles pulled the parchment, folded and unfolded so many times it was fraying along the lines, from his inner coat pocket.

He tried not to stare at the cracks in her skin, black lines that encroached from her hairline and jaw, marring her otherwise smooth coppery complexion. She took the letter with slender fingers, pointed nails scraping gently across his skin.

"How long has she been gone?" Derek asked.

Charles turned with him, and the two led the way across the courtyard and up the stone steps. The guards followed them at a respectful distance.

"I'm not sure," Charles replied, his stomach clenching. "Her sister sent the letter. Depending on when it got here, anywhere from a few days to a week."

"Yes," the witch said from behind them. "She seems quite concerned. Rash decision by the king. They know little about this Lord Gadrel."

"Have you heard of him, Sym?" Derek asked.

The three stepped into the gaping palace entrance hall. Charles glanced at his brother as the stewards on either side of the door bowed low. It was the sort of thing Derek would have been used to, but the attention was still an itch against Charles's nerves.

Derek seemed entirely unbothered.

The witch shook her head in response to his question. She reached up and Charles noticed, for the first time, that a small grey mouse stood on her shoulder. She scratched behind its ear. "No. At least, not by that name."

Charles gave her a sharp look. "You think he is using a false identity?"

"Not necessarily," she said. "When one's life is prolonged with the use of magic, it becomes easy to change who you are as generations pass."

Derek raised an eyebrow. "You didn't have a name when we met."

She folded the letter, handed it back to Charles, and brushed a lock of black hair behind her shoulder. "I'd forgotten it. That's not the same as not having one."

After food and a quick bath for Derek and Sym, Charles gathered them both into his private study and pulled out a map.

"Here is the capital of Faytrue." He leaned on the table. Happy to have his brother back, happy to have help in the form of a powerful witch, yet still incredibly anxious and desperate to get going. "Riva's sister said they were headed here." He pointed to a sliver of land between Faytrue and the neighboring kingdom to the east.

"The Hidden Hamlet," Derek said with a nod.

Charles frowned at his brother. "You know it?"

Derek shrugged. "Father had a close eye on the land when the Continent War was on. It was part of brokering the peace treaty."

"Both countries agreed to leave it a hamlet instead of trying to extend their borders."

Derek nodded. "It was that or keep fighting over a handful of villages and some woods half the size of Lagonia."

"Right. Well," Charles continued. "Apparently this Lord Gadrel hails from the Hamlet. Supposedly, he rules it."

"The sister's letter suggested great ambition," Sym murmured from the edge of the table. "Ambition can be dangerous in the hands of powerful men."

Silence followed her words, and Charles couldn't help the rush of cold that went through his body. The urge to leave, to get on a ship and sail to Faytrue without hesitation, filled him.

He even took half a step toward the door before Derek spoke again.

"All right, brother. We have a wizard, a not-quite kingdom far from our own, and a kidnapped princess."

Charles met his brother's gaze. Derek's serious concern slid into a mischievous smile much like their late mother's.

Charles nodded, clenching his hands at his sides with the strain of standing still.

"Only one question remains."

Sym took a step toward them. A sly smile crept across her face as she looked at Derek.

Derek put a hand on Charles's shoulder. "How do we get you out of the castle?"

Chapter Ten

A Maid and an Embrace

"A reverse heist." Sym chortled. "How exciting."

Derek stifled a snort as the two hurried down a dark corridor toward Charles's royal quarters. They'd once belonged to Derek, and he had found it a bit disorienting to go to Charles's old rooms to rest a few hours before they left. He could only imagine the struggle Charles had dealt with for the past month.

A tiny squeak drew his attention to Greggory, perched on Sym's shoulder and firmly clutching her driftwood (he hoped, because if not it was likely bone) earring.

"Indeed, Greggory," Sym said with excitement in her voice. "Great punishment if we are caught. Kidnapping a crown prince is highly frowned upon."

Derek sighed but glanced behind to check that no one had seen them. "No one would think we're kidnapping my brother. But given how my father reacted to my little ocean escapade, it's better to leave while the guards are asleep."

Sym cackled. Derek shushed her. She stuck out her tongue, and Greggory did the same.

With another sigh, cut by the entertained grin on his face, Derek continued down the hall until they reached Charles's rooms. He rapt softly on the door.

It opened almost immediately, and Derek had to wheel away, stuffing his knuckles into his mouth to stop from laughing loud enough to wake the entire palace.

"Shut it," Charles snapped.

"I don't know if that tone fits," Sym said mildly, gesturing at him.

The crown prince of Cerulean was dressed as a maid. The end of his sword protruded from the multi-layers of skirts. The apron had been tied rather poorly. His dark head of hair was disguised with a borrowed blonde wig that flopped down around his shoulders. Only his face would give him away.

"Can you do something about all that?" Derek asked with a wave at his brother's stubbled jaw. He snorted at the murderous look Charles gave him.

Sym nodded and, with a brush of her long, sharp fingernails across Charles's cheek, his features shifted and became more feminine.

Barely a moment later the three of them were striding quickly through the wide yet maze-like palace halls.

"Your guards?" Sym whispered as they rounded a corner.

"Still at their posts," Charles replied with half a shrug. "Well, asleep at their posts. I expect there's someone at the base of my windows, but the men inside enjoyed that tea you gave me." He raised an eyebrow at Derek. "They'll be all right, won't they?"

Derek's mouth twitched up at the corner. "I was worried my first time using it too, but Sym promises there are no lasting ill effects. And so far, she's been right."

"*So far*," Sym hissed with derision. "Humph."

At her shoulder, Greggory let out an admonishing squeak.

***

"Nearly there," Derek muttered, the humor of the situation a bit diffused as they neared the exit. They'd already passed more than enough guards to put him on edge.

A few had recognized him with a nod or salute. None, fortunately, had seemed to give maid-Charles or Sym a second glance.

"Derek!"

He froze, recognizing his father's voice as a pool of familiar anxiety splashed in his stomach.

"Keep going," he hissed to his brother and Sym. He turned.

King Victor strode down the main hall towards the three of them. He was regal as ever, even in a warm robe and soft slippers. His gaze followed Sym and Charles as they continued on to the doors.

"My son," Victor said upon his approach, and Derek was surprised to see a warm smile.

He'd thought they were caught.

"Father," Derek said with a suitable bow. He hesitated, unsure of what to say at this late hour with his pajama-clad father.

"You're leaving again?" The king gestured to the fresh set of gear on Derek's person.

He'd replaced his jacket and boots for a newer pair. The sword at his side was sharpened, the scabbard wrapped with an extra layer of leather. Sym and Charles carried the bags, as would be appropriate if a strange woman and a maid were traveling with a prince.

"Yes." Derek looked up. "I'm off to Faytrue."

"Ahh, Charles's princess?"

Derek nodded, his expression tight as a combination of emotions battled inside him. It was a relief, having such freedom from the palace. Yet he very much missed the long conversations he used to have with the king. As different as they were, and as strained as their relationship often was because of the burden on Derek, they had once been quite close.

Victor put a hand on Derek's shoulder. "Your brother will be angry about not going, but I know you'll do what's right for him. It's just..." He hesitated. "It's not safe."

Derek's brow pinched in a slight furrow.

Victor grimaced. "What I mean is, it's not safe—"

"For the heir," Derek cut him off.

The king removed his hand, clenching it into a fist at his side. "Yes."

The word burrowed into Derek's chest, sending an ache through his heart.

"You should know," Victor continued, his voice tight with an emotion Derek couldn't quite place. "I don't want you going either. But your brother would lose his mind if we sent a squadron of soldiers instead. When he said you were coming—" He broke off with a sigh. "He trusts you, and I do as well."

The words should have eased the heartache, but they didn't. Derek nodded.

"And be sure you return after. Not for a drop off of the princess, but for a proper visit. Your sisters miss you."

Derek swallowed, overly aware that his brother and friend were waiting outside, perhaps already at the stables or even further. "I'll be back, Father."

Victor reached out, his hand brushing Derek's arm before he took a step and pulled his son into an embrace.

Derek was stiff for a second, confused and befuddled. Then he caught the old familiar scent of candlewood and pine and just a hint of mint. Emotion choked his throat as a wave of memories that no longer belonged to both of them crashed against him.

He looped his arms around his father, careful to angle away from where his sword hung at his side, and squeezed back.

They broke the hug a moment later. Derek cleared his throat, blinking away the tears in his eyes as his father bade him goodnight and turned to make his way back into the depth of the castle.

Derek stood a moment, sifting through the emotions within before he gave himself a shake, straightened his back, and hurried after his companions.

CHAPTER ELEVEN

Wishing

Riva's well-crafted leather shoes were silent on the stairs of the inn. She'd sat awake for the last hour, perched on the edge of her bed with nerves hammering her heart and plans racing through her mind.

The first step was getting out of the inn. Getting far enough away that she could breathe and settle her heavy anxiety.

Britta had given the gentle knock. The light under Lord Gadrel's door was dark. Silence and patience were key now.

Riva reached the bottom of the steps. She looped the small bag of provisions from the innkeeper over her shoulder and hurried to the front door. It was unlocked. She silently promised to return one day with many gifts to thank Britta and pushed. It opened with a slight creak, and she halted for a few breathless seconds.

Nothing stirred in the darkness of the inn, and with careful footsteps, she slid out the door and closed it behind her.

The cold of the night was a welcome break from the hot tension she'd been carrying in her back. She swallowed, glanced at the windows above, and then broke into a quiet run.

She passed the horseless carriage, passed the little wooden fence that lined the drive and marked the property of Britta and her husband, and was a few paces from the main road when she was jerked to a stop by a hard pull at the back of her head.

Riva let out a yelp of pain, groaned, and staggered back. She swung furiously at whoever had grabbed her, but her hands met nothing.

She froze. Her eyes widened, a new horror sinking into her bones. Her hair. Her hair had stopped her, yanked her backward hard enough to wrench her neck at a painful angle. She stared at her long golden locks, fresh betrayal bubbling in her chest.

Then she noted the silver cuffs. Still fixed in her hair but hovering in the air instead of dangling at her shoulders. They glinted in the moonlight. No. She glanced up at a towering pine blocking the sky from view. They glinted in the darkness, silver runes glowing with some kind of magic.

Riva let out a shuddering breath. It wasn't her hair trying to keep her there; it was the gift she'd received from Gadrel. She only needed to remove them and freedom would be within reach. She took hold of the cuffs.

Only a split second later she released them, cursing under her breath as stinging welts grew across her palms.

"Not smart," a voice said behind her.

She turned, forced to step toward the cuffs to give herself room to move while they still clutched her hair.

A familiar shadow moved through the trees at the side of the road. Riva almost spat as Lord Gadrel sauntered toward her.

"And not lady-like, that mouth of yours."

Riva's lips curled into a scowl, the heated fury in her almost making her forget the pain in her hands.

"What's not smart?" she demanded in a hoarse whisper. "Running?"

Gadrel sneered. "Touching magic when you don't know what it does."

Riva inhaled through flared nostrils. The reality of her immobility sank a pit of fear right through her fiery anger. She took another step back, toward the inn, and the cuffs dropped.

The sudden weight of her hair hurt. She let out a soft cry and went to touch her scalp, but her fingertips were blistered as well, and that pain was more intense.

"Get these off of me," Riva said in a low, regal tone. "Now."

Gadrel tutted. "You don't give *me* orders, Princess. I tried to do this the nice way, but if you're going to dishonor your family and the deal we made—"

"I made no deal," she spat.

"Your father did," Gadrel snapped. "And you will honor it, whether you chose to or not."

Riva snarled. "I will *not* marry you."

Gadrel shook his head, casting his gaze at the sky for a moment before he met her gaze. "You don't have to turn this into a punishment, Riva. This could be a good thing for both of us."

"No good comes from buying a person, Lord Gadrel."

Her words were laced with icy poison that she desperately wished was literal. Why couldn't she be a witch from the old stories? Dangerous, powerful, capable. Instead, she was locked to her power, unable to cut herself free and now even more caged by the damned cuffs she'd so foolishly accepted.

The wizard shrugged. "See it how you will, princess. The situation will not change, no matter what common folk friends you make along the way."

He strode past her, headed back toward the inn. She turned to follow his movements with wary eyes.

"You'll have a better trip tomorrow if you sleep tonight," he called over his shoulder. "And, perhaps think twice before you accept gifts from people you've insulted."

Riva stood rigid as he opened the door to the inn and disappeared inside. Tears burned at first, then froze as they rolled down her cheeks and were hit by the cold night air. Her hands, red and sore, throbbed as she clutched them to her chest.

Helplessness seeped into her bones, dragging her down and rooting her to the spot. What was to be done? She was trapped. Caged by the very reason Gadrel wanted her in the first place.

She glanced down at the silver cuffs now dangling innocently at her chest. They no longer glowed. She prodded one with a tentative finger and nothing happened. She doubted they'd remain inert if she tried to remove them.

Riva turned from the inn, staring out at the dark road. She closed her eyes and imagined, so desperately it seemed odd that it wouldn't come true, seeing a horse galloping toward her. She envisioned Charles, sweaty from the road, dismounting and running to her side. She almost felt his arms around her, holding her close as he whispered his love in her ear and promised they'd find a way out of this together.

But when she opened her eyes the road remained empty, the cuffs remained on, and her hands remained red and blistered.

Riva shook her head. She knew better. Change didn't come from wishing.

She gritted her teeth and looked down at her hair. The number of times it had gotten her in trouble were beyond count. But there were occasions, rare as they were, when it actually helped.

She spoke to it, her voice soft in the darkness. "Remember that day Benji found a bird's nest up a tree? He climbed too high and fell. Remember how we got to him first and it was the worst thing we'd ever seen? His leg bent all funny, all that blood coming from his head?" Riva swallowed and ran her aching fingers through the bottom strands of her hair. "I was so worried, but you fixed him. Do you remember that?"

Almost in answer, the tips of her hair began to glow with a soft golden light. Different from the protective magic that flared at inopportune times, this was gentle. A cool sensation eased over her palms. The blisters shrank. The pain faded.

Riva returned to the inn, trudged up the stairs, and quietly closed herself in her room. She would go with Gadrel tomorrow. The thought of the cuffs doing permanent damage, or the wizard harming Britta and her family if Riva didn't do as he said, didn't seem unlikely.

She went to a small set of shelves in the corner of the room. There were three books collecting dust. She plucked the smallest one, a novel of poetry, and began flipping through the pages.

She had no ink, but maybe she didn't need any.

Chapter Twelve

Brotherly Conversations

The excitement of successfully escaping the palace and making it to the harbor of Lagonia with no royal guards on their tail, nor in fact anything to suggest someone had found out that Charles was gone, was muted by the enormity of the task before them.

Charles sat on an upturned crate staring at the water through the gaps in the dock. Sunrise approached. With it would come another day Riva was in the clutches of this Lord Gadrel. This wizard from a strip of land not associated with any kingdom. A variable that would make solving the problem with diplomacy rather difficult.

Charles blew a strand of his wig out of his face and glanced toward the ship at the end of the dock. Derek was negotiating passage with the captain. With any luck they'd be at the shore of Faytrue within two days. Avoiding the capital city was the hard part; it was the main port and hub through which most ships traded. Instead, they'd head east along the coast until they reached the smaller harbor near the border of Faytrue.

From there they'd get horses. And they'd rescue Riva.

Charles's stomach churned. He had such limited information. Even combing through his father's notes about the state of the Hidden Hamlet after the war gave him little to work with. Lord Gadrel had been around then, over a decade ago. Upon inspection of the documents from those days, done in secret the night before Derek had arrived, it became clear that Gadrel's decision to remain impartial was not a philanthropic one. He had demanded that both nations recognize his Hamlet as a country of its own, with him as king. When they refused, he'd refused to join the war, on either side.

"They'll take us," Derek said in a low voice as he stooped to sit beside Charles on the crate. "It's already expensive, but it'll cost an armful of gold if they find out who you are."

Charles sighed. He'd figured as much. "I don't mind the skirts," he grumbled. "But the wig itches."

Derek chuckled. "You can stay in our room most of the trip. If we have fair winds—"

"Two days," Charles cut in. "I know." He swallowed.

Derek put a hand on his forearm, brow furrowed as he met Charles's eye with a hard look. "We'll get her back. I promise you."

Charles's mouth twitched. "Still the big brother."

Derek scoffed and waved away the words. "You'd do the same for me."

"I did." Charles raised an eyebrow, and Derek shrugged.

"I suppose." Derek stretched. "But I'm not sure I'd weigh getting me out of the palace on the same scale with going on a full-bore rescue mission."

Charles gaped. "I'd have come. I'd have come in a minute if you'd—"

He broke off as his brother fell into a fit of laughter. Charles rolled his eyes and shoved Derek. The former crown prince nearly fell off the crates as Sym walked up, giving both of them a bemused expression.

"What hilarity did I miss?"

"Nothing," Charles grumbled as Derek continued his belly-deep laugh. "Just my brother's usual jokes."

Sym nodded solemnly. "I did not think he was capable of being funny the first time we met. But he has proved me wrong on more than one occasion."

In the darkness, Charles thought he saw the faint outline of Greggory shaking his head on her shoulder.

"In my defense," Derek said after a deep inhale. "I was quite concerned about my fiancé being dead, and the rumors about you didn't paint a comedic picture."

Sym rolled her eyes. "Rumors are not the standard by which to judge."

"I know that now," Derek mumbled, looking appropriately chagrined.

A stir of sympathy rolled through Charles's chest. "In my brother's defense, if we listened to half the stories about witches growing up, he wouldn't have come anywhere near you, dead fiancé or not."

Sym tilted her head, dark eyes glinting in the low torchlight that lined the dock. "I'll be interested to hear these stories during our trip."

Charles's eyes widened, and he exchanged a mildly concerned look with his brother. If Derek and Sym hadn't already talked about the many awful things most people thought about witches, he didn't want to be there when the conversation finally happened.

"We should get on the ship," Derek said with a half-cough.

They were close. According to the captain, they'd arrive in the morning. They'd made almost disturbingly good time. Charles suspected Sym had something to do with their fair winds.

He'd told them about Riva's power that first night on the ship. The odd way her hair sometimes glowed, sometimes acted of its own accord to do things normal people couldn't dream of. When he'd told them of the reaction from Riva's family about her abilities, Sym had excused herself for nearly an hour. Even after she'd returned, the vibration of her anger was palpable in the air.

"How does Father talk to you?"

Charles took his gaze from the dark wooden panels above him and looked left to where his brother lay beside him.

Charles had been awake for hours, his stomach tight with worry, his mind whirling with possible outcomes of their mission. Sym's soft snores from above told him the witch was asleep. He'd thought Derek was as well.

"What do you mean?"

Derek shifted, turning to meet Charles's gaze in the dark of their bunk. "Father. There's something... different about the way he spoke to me."

"Shouldn't there be?" Charles moved as well, leaning back against the bulkhead to give some room for them to look at each other. "You're not crown prince any longer."

His brother sighed. "I know, and I expected to have less conversation, less contact. But he seemed regretful about it. As though he wanted me in the palace." He let out a bitter huff of a laugh. "Even as crown prince I rarely felt that."

Charles nodded and leaned up on his elbow, resting his head on his hand. "There have been a few changes while you've been gone, Derek."

Derek was quiet.

Charles continued, attempting a tone that didn't suggest any sort of animosity, "I don't know if it escaped your attention or not, and it would be no mark against you if it did, but Father rarely had time for the rest of our siblings. I was lucky to catch a few kind words when I was in Lagonia. It was part of the draw of traveling as often as possible."

Derek swallowed.

"Well," Charles went on. "The little ones deserve better than that, so I instituted some changes. I was fortunate with the timing. I had Father's good favor from finding a bride so quickly after everything with Lady Lydia. We've been doing family dinners once a week." He smiled in the darkness, trying to put some levity into his words. "The twins don't much care for them, but the girls seem keen. They've enjoyed the time with Father, and it's forced him to notice them."

"I..." Derek hesitated, shifting in the bed.

The creak of the ship, the sloshing of water against the wood, and the soft, sleepy squeaks from Greggory filled what would have been silence between the brothers.

"Mother used to do it," Charles said softly. "She'd make sure Father paid attention to us. When she died—"

"I should have stepped up." Derek's voice was tight. "I should have—"

"Father," Charles interrupted, "should have behaved as a father. He was grieving. We all were, but that doesn't give him an excuse. His failures are not your fault."

Derek hesitated then let out a low laugh. "You've mastered a key part of crown princing, brother."

Charles snorted, the abrupt shift humoring him. "Explain?"

"Courtiers, ambassadors, visiting royals, they have a habit of spiraling over one thing or another. You've just done a wonderful job of stopping me doing the same."

Charles shifted onto his back with a chuckle. He stared up at the planks of wood, and his thoughts turned to his love.

"Riva is like that," he murmured.

He felt, rather than saw, his brother copy his movement. The two lay on the narrow cot in the late hours of the night, talking in a way they hadn't done since they were boys.

"Tell me about her," Derek said, his voice soft.

Charles grinned. "She stops me spiraling. Her voice… Your lady—"

"Lydia was never mine," Derek interrupted.

Charles rolled his eyes. "*The* lady, her voice is something to behold because of its beauty. She has a rare gift and a marvelous power."

"Indeed."

"Riva is like that as well. Not her magic, or how her voice sounds…" Charles broke off with a frustrated sigh. He wasn't explaining it properly. Yet Derek waited quietly.

"When she speaks," Charles finally continued, "people listen. Noble-born, common folk, everyone. Her kindness breaks through every barrier."

Derek let out a low whistle. "You're madly in love, brother."

A loud laugh burst from Charles. Derek elbowed him.

"Sorry," Charles said, still stifling his laughter. "Only, I'd thought that was obvious by now."

"What, because we snuck you out of the castle, chartered a ship across the channel, and are headed to fight a wizard for her hand? I mean, if that's enough evidence for *you*..."

Both of them broke into fits of laughter so loud they woke Sym. When the witch swung her head upside down over the side of the bunk to scold them, they laughed even harder.

CHAPTER THIRTEEN

A Charming Village

Riva and Gadrel passed the border of Faytrue the day after leaving Britta's inn. Having a carriage that didn't require rest for the horses sped up the trip considerably. A fact that Riva swallowed down like a bitter concoction.

The cuffs were still locked in place, holding her hair and power hostage. She steadfastly ignored Lord Gadrel during the trek. Part of her wanted to punish him with the silence. Another part knew nothing she said would change his actions. And a third, strongest part threatened to explode with rage if she so much as opened her lips.

"The Hidden Hamlet," he said as the carriage rumbled across a stone bridge. A steadily running river spanned either direction. The natural eastern barrier of Faytrue's territory.

Riva looked out the window in spite of herself, and the pit in her stomach deepened. Though the river should have fed the soil on both sides, the Hamlet was dry. Dusty, baren land stretched as far as she could see. She glanced out the other side, attempting to be discreet, and it was entirely the same. Not a green thing, not even grass, to be seen for miles. Perhaps it was the lifeless nature of her surroundings that made her so tired.

"What happened to this place?" she asked, forgetting her vow of silence in the face of such a stark difference after merely crossing a bridge.

"Whatever do you mean?"

Riva tried to read Gadrel's tone as she met his gaze. Sarcastic, but something else as well. She couldn't place it and chose to ignore him rather than respond to such a ridiculous question.

A few minutes later, however, she couldn't help herself.

"How far are we from your... town, or city, or wherever you live?"

He fixed his grey eyes on her. Grey... though she'd sworn they'd been black the day before. His hair had changed a bit as well. She hadn't noticed while trying so hard to ignore him. The salt and pepper was more salt, the edges, especially around his ears, definitely greyer than they'd been previously.

"My home is just past the village."

Riva gritted her teeth. "What do your people think? Of you stealing a princess from a sovereign nation?"

He chuckled. The sound was hoarse and turned into a slight cough before he cleared his throat and answered. "My people do as I command. And I didn't steal you, Princess Rivanissee." He leaned in, the lines around his eyes in sharp focus even as Riva backed against her seat. "I bought you, remember?"

She snarled. Magic or no, she was tempted to leap across the carriage and throttle him with her bare hands.

He must have sensed it, or she was staring at his neck too much, because he laughed and dragged a hand across his throat. "You wouldn't get far, Princess. You've barely seen a touch of the power I possess."

"It doesn't matter," she murmured. Though her chest still burned with rage, she inhaled, easing her fury. She thought back to the small book of poetry she'd found at the inn. The message she'd left with a heartfelt hope that Charles would find it. Find her.

Gadrel's gaze darkened. "Doesn't matter?"

"Your magic," Riva said, her voice quiet now as she turned her thoughts to her love. "It doesn't matter how powerful you are."

"You're wrong." He turned to face the window, and Riva was glad for the silence.

❧ ☙

They arrived at the village barely two hours later, reminding Riva exactly how small the Hamlet was. The strip of land was narrower than the channel to get from Charles's kingdom to hers. She estimated it would only take another two hours to arrive at the neighboring border crossing if they continued on.

The carriage rumbled to a stop. Even the road here was rocky and hard, not the smooth packed dirt and cobblestone she was used to. They'd passed a collection of seemingly empty small homes and shabby buildings before pulling up at the village square.

She stepped out to a sea of faces and nerves alight in her belly.

The entire village had to be there, over a hundred people standing idly in the square. They chatted amongst each other. Children darted here and there.

Riva glanced around and noted the older structures, well cared-for but weathered. A dry fountain stood on a slightly raised dais in the center of the square. Signs on the buildings around them marked an inn, a tavern, a butcher, bakery, grocers... all the normal things one would expect to find in a quaint village.

Yet her stomach churned.

Lord Gadrel stepped out of the carriage behind her, his footsteps crunching on the hard ground. Her gaze snapped toward him and back to the villagers. They'd turned their attention from her, and their low murmuring had gone silent. Even the children had ceased their scampering.

"Greetings, my Lord." A tall man stepped forward from the crowd. If the braided patterning to his ruddy hair and beard were any match in meaning to the northern regions of Faytrue, he was a leader of the village.

He stooped into a low bow. Riva's lip curled before she caught herself and smoothed her expression. She looked out into the crowd and noted that hers was not the only angry reaction. Many of the faces behind the man were poorly disguised; smiles covered glinting fear or fury beneath. A middle-aged woman glared openly, her arms folded over her chest.

"Ian, good man." Gadrel moved to the man and put a hand on his arm.

Only when the lord touched him did Ian rise from his bow. Gadrel raised an eyebrow, and Ian turned to wave a hand over the heads of the villagers. In unison, they also bowed low.

Riva swallowed.

"Riva."

She flinched at Gadrel's voice. He beckoned and, with a grimace, she stepped toward him.

"This is Havita, the shining heart of the Hidden Hamlet."

Riva gave a gentle nod. The villagers were still bowed.

"What do you think of my little village?" Gadrel asked, a smug grin on his aged face.

Her gaze darted to Ian, who stood still and silent, his face guarded, and his arms clasped behind his back.

"It's..." Riva hesitated. Still, the people had not risen. The anxiety in her stomach shifted to fear. "It's lovely. I especially like the trees."

It was true, Havita boasted the first greenery she'd seen since they crossed the border. The few scraggly bushes and thin trees added texture to the landscape. In the distance, against the horizon beyond the village, a towering set of dense evergreens suggested a forest had somehow survived this desolate place.

"Good." Gadrel nodded to Ian.

The man cleared his throat.

The sound was low but must have been some kind of sign. The villagers straightened as one and began to move away. They broke off into small groupings, some hurrying toward the businesses, others meandering slowly, and a few hovering around the fountain, eyeing Riva, Gadrel, and Ian as the two men began a conversation.

Riva stood silent, watching the villagers and confirming her own suspicions and fears about Lord Gadrel's manner with the way they skirted around the carriage.

"How fairs my town?" Gadrel's voice, coarse and throaty, carried through the bustling square.

His attention was still on Ian, but Riva noted a handful of glares at his words. The woman who had not bothered to cover her expression stalked to the inn, watching them from the doorway for a moment before moving inside.

"Well, Lord Gadrel. Things are well." The man's large green eyes flicked to Riva and back. "I gather your trip to Faytrue was successful."

"Indeed," Gadrel said with a twisted smile. "Riva, meet Ian. Ian, this is Princess Rivanissee of Faytrue."

Riva swallowed down her disgust but did not bother to hide her twinge as Gadrel's hand landed on her shoulder. She stepped away from him, and he scowled.

"You are the leader of this village?" She directed her attention to Ian, who cast a rapid glance at Gadrel before nodding.

"I am, Princess. We are glad to have you. If my lord wishes it, we can begin wedding preparations immediately."

A shudder ran down Riva's spine, and her mind raced. Her first instinct was to correct him. She'd not be marrying Lord Gadrel—immediately or otherwise. However, the way the townsfolk reacted to him, the way Ian stood tense and alert, the way the cuffs dragged at her hair as a constant reminder of the magical chains binding her...

She had yet to experience Gadrel angry around others. The safe move, the smart move, would be to remain neutral until a chance to escape without getting other people hurt presented itself.

So, she changed the subject. "I like the greenery you have here." Riva gestured to the scraggly oak that grew up and over the dry fountain. "I'm sure they are beautiful in the spring."

Ian shot another glance at Gadrel before turning to look at the square as well. "Indeed, we often have a variety of colors in Havita. In the spring and autumn as well."

"And the winter? Is there snow this far south?"

Ian chuckled. The sound was rich and deep. "We get one or two snowfalls a year, but nothing compared to the storms up north. My people are from a village at the base of the mountains. My grandparents often told stories of terrible storms that went on for months at a time."

Riva grinned. "I love the snow, but I've always found those sorts of storms terrifying. My family has a home near the old Ogre fortress of Nexintrum." She shivered. "I never understood how trappers made a living until I realized how many furs were needed to keep me warm during winters there."

The village leader matched her expression, gesturing to the trees. "It's a lovely sight when the rising sun catches the snow on the branches."

"Are my rooms prepared?"

The interruption startled them both. Riva faced Gadrel, working to keep her expression from falling. His words would not have that kind of power over her.

"Rooms?" she asked. "I thought your home was near."

Gadrel eyed her a moment before nodding. "It is. But the forest is dangerous to traverse at night."

Riva's lip curled into a bitter smile. "Even for *such* a powerful wizard?"

His brow furrowed and anger lit across his face. "Even for me, Princess. It isn't safe."

Ian moved into Gadrel's view. "Your rooms are ready, my lord. We've had them waiting for your return."

He gestured, and Gadrel turned and strode toward the inn without another word.

Riva hesitated.

The cuffs in her hair bounced lightly, in the direction of the one who controlled them. With a scowl, Riva followed them.

CHAPTER FOURTEEN

A Melancholy Trek

Derek trotted along a few paces behind his brother's horse. The air was crisp, the sun shining, and the sky clear. It ought to have been a beautiful morning. But Charles's melancholy was infectious.

Or perhaps the weight on Derek's chest came from the realization that in four weeks Charles had done more to care for their siblings than Derek had done in all the years since their mother's death. Their conversation on the ship strayed through his thoughts every hour or so, and he spent far too long pondering what he might have done differently and why it was he hadn't noticed just how closed off his father had become.

A squeak drew his attention from falling into those thoughts yet again. He glanced down.

Greggory sat on the horse's mane, his oddly intelligent eyes fixed on Derek.

The latter let out a sigh. "I still don't speak mouse, little fella."

A chuckle preceded Sym kicking up beside him. Her horse was not a purchased one. She'd called it from the ocean again when they'd docked in the harbor. Derek couldn't be certain, but he was fairly confident it was the same horse. Somehow. It had all the same markings and still smelled of fish.

"He said to be at ease. He doesn't smell predators near."

"Ahh." Derek gave a cordial, if lightly skeptical nod. "Thank you, Greggory."

The little grey mouse bobbed his head and returned his attention to the gap between the horse's ears where, Derek assumed, he was watching the road ahead.

"You're not worried about attackers?" Sym stared at him, her big dark eyes fixed on him and ignoring the road entirely.

He huffed out a chuckle.

"Not here. We're still deep enough within Faytrue's borders. It's good to stay alert, but I'll have a weapon out when we get closer to the outskirts."

She pursed her lips and nodded. "How much longer?"

"Another few hours to the town closest to the border." Charles called from ahead of them. "We will have to spend the night."

Empathy flared in Derek at the tight edge to Charles's voice.

"It's too dangerous to cut across the border in the dark. We should be able to reach Riva... We should reach the Hamlet tomorrow."

Derek exchanged a side-glance with Sym, then urged his horse forward to ride alongside his brother.

"Tonight will be for planning then?" he asked.

Charles frowned at him. "What is there to plan? We get there and get Riva back."

Derek gave a rueful smile. "I hope it is that easy, brother. But something tells me a wizard willing to travel so far for a girl with magic hair might have ulterior motives."

"His motives don't matter to me," Charles growled.

"They matter to me. They will play a role in how difficult it may be to get your beloved back. I wore that crown for a while before you did, Charles. Let me lend a bit of my experience with situations like these."

"Situations like—" Charles broke off with a snort. "Derek, you abandoned your responsibilities to go on a half-cocked quest into the ocean to rescue a woman you knew for three days. What part of that was planned?"

Derek gave a grudging nod. "All right. That's fair. But before that, I had an established record of levelheaded planning."

Charles's lips curled into a tense smile. "I know. I'm glad to have you by my side for this. I should have..." His hand tightened into a fist around the reins. "I should have sent for her sooner. The minute that shell broke."

Derek's stomach clenched at the pain so clear on his brother's face. "There was a lot going on in those moments and the preceding days."

"I wrote as soon as I could." He looked at Derek, eyes glistening with tears, then his head fell. "I didn't mean for this to happen."

"Charles." Derek wheeled his horse around, forcing his brother to come to a halt. "This isn't your fault. No part of what happened is because of anything you did or didn't do. We don't know if Riva's father would have accepted your offer. We don't know if the wizard had his sights set on her before I even left to get Lady Lydia."

He ducked his head, forcing Charles to meet his gaze. "We're getting her back. You love her, and she loves you, and that would be enough. But since you've also got me." He patted the sword at his side. "And a magical sea witch who has a particular issue with people who think they can buy someone..."

Sym accompanied his words with a snarl that showed her sharp teeth.

Derek grinned. "You've got power behind you, Charles. Never mind that you're crown prince of Cerulean. True love and anger. That's what will get this done."

Charles huffed out a breath through flared nostrils. Then he nodded.

The three continued on, only a few miles between them and their evening rest. A rest which would be less sleep, and more planning a rescue.

⁂

"Welcome." A stout woman with a wide smile that didn't reach her sad eyes greeted them at the inn on the far edge of town. She had her son stable the horses—he gave Sym's a not-subtle sniff as he led them away—and brought them all inside for a warm meal and a set of rooms for the night.

Derek handled the business of inquiries and finances. Charles had a distant look in his eye as he followed Sym to the hearth, and he sat staring into the flames for several long minutes before picking up his bowl of stew.

"Two rooms, please." Derek fished four silvers from his pocket, then added a gold piece to the pile.

The woman's brow furrowed. She looked at him, taking closer stock of his clothes, face, and companions.

"And some information, if you have any," Derek continued quietly.

The innkeeper scowled. "My husband helps run things in town. There's nothing worth stealing there. Not even the mayor has more than a nice home to his name."

Derek blinked, confusion freezing him for a brief second. "I'm... sorry. What?"

"You're pirates, aren't you?" She inhaled, taking half a step back even though a full countertop already separated them. "You'd have to be, coming in dressed like you are, flashing about those sorts of weapons, that kind of gold."

"It's one—" Derek broke off, shook his head, and started again. "We aren't pirates. Though I understand the confusion. My brother and I, and our friend, are traveling from a... distant kingdom. His fiancé, the love of his life, has been taken. We are on a quest of sorts. To save her."

To Derek's surprise, the woman's face lit with understanding.

"Charles?" she murmured, casting a glance toward the fire.

Derek frowned. "How did you—"

"She was here." The woman hurried around the counter, leaving the coins where they lay, and hurried toward Sym and Charles. "Riva."

Charles stood so quickly a chunk of his stew sloshed onto the stone in front of the fire with a hiss. "You've seen her?" he demanded, looking from the innkeeper to Derek and back. "When?"

The woman opened her mouth, hesitated, and then grimaced. "I'm sorry, Highness. I've gotten all giddy and forgotten myself. I shouldn't talk of—"

Charles cut her off with a glare at Derek. "You told her who we are?"

"No," Derek replied with an eye roll. "I didn't."

"I know who you are, assuming this man is telling the truth about your intentions."

Derek pinched the bridge of his nose. A throbbing had started in his temple. "Let's slow this down, shall we? I'm Derek. This is Charles and Sym. Who are you? And how do you know Riva?"

"I'm Britta. And I'll tell you everything I know about the princess, as long as you swear to me you're after her for good reasons."

"True love?" Sym asked, her voice mild.

Britta glanced her way, and it must have been her first up-close look because she startled and gaped for a second. Then she composed herself and nodded. "You are the one then," she said to Charles. "The love she spoke of. She knew you'd come."

Derek's heart ached. Charles's lips trembled, the tears in his eyes reflecting the light from the fire.

"I came. What do you know? How far ahead are they?"

CHAPTER FIFTEEN

An Ocean Apart

Two Years Ago

Charles hurried off the ship. His sea legs wobbled on the deck; it had been a long voyage. A long time since he'd seen Riva's face.

He slung his pack across his shoulder, waved to the captain of his favorite ship, and jogged away toward the city center of Faytrue's capital. It was hard to believe he'd only met the princess once. Their letters for the past six months had begun simply, hesitant. But as they'd become more comfortable with one another, their messages had grown more intimate.

Now, after six months traveling, Charles's heart was in his throat at the idea of seeing her face again.

They'd agreed to meet in the bustling marketplace. If she could get away from the palace.

He crossed his fingers as he strode down the dirty cobblestone streets. They became cleaner and wider as he neared the city center. Eventually, wide thoroughfares lined with pleasant brick homes and apartments became the standard. And, after a short time, they were replaced with storefronts, inns, and taverns.

He came upon the market and was startled by how few stalls there were. Perhaps it was still early, or the city was still recovering from the war. Riva had spoken of the crown's financial troubles with little detail in case their letters were intercepted.

Still, the small number of folks shopping made it easy to spot her.

She'd have been easy to find anyway. Her light was like the first rays of sunshine after a long, dark night.

Charles let out a breath, his heartbeat quickening at the sight of her. He couldn't control the smile that split his lips.

She was dressed plainly, not in anything like the court gown he'd seen at their initial introduction. Her long golden locks were braided into two sections, looped around and over to create a woven design that hung low on each side of her head. Pale lilac skirts and a sage green bodice accented the flowers she'd used to decorate her braids.

She wore no crown. Another similarity between the two of them that livened the emotion in his chest.

He picked up his pace, watching with excitement as she spotted him. Her brilliant blue eyes widened. Her lips formed a smile that stole his breath all over again.

Present Day

Golden locks as fair as spring
The ache of love and yearning
Towers high and valleys low
Could not keep me from your glow
To fight for stones makes one a knave
To fight for you, is all I crave

***

Dark as embers in the morn
Your love a voice beyond all scorn
Though oceans stretch between us now
I'll see you again, this I vow
To run away takes strength of a kind
To run to you, my only mind

***

"What is this?" Derek asked.

Charles clenched the poem in his hand, turning the old paper into a wrinkled ball. Riva had ripped it from a book in her room, folded it gently, and passed it into Britta's hand before she'd left. The innkeeper had handed it over. Along with the reassuring news that Riva and the wizard were only a few days ahead of them. They'd saved a lot of time taking the ship east.

"It's ours." Charles swallowed; his jaw was clenched so tight it caused his neck to ache. "Our promise to each other. We each found it in a collection of old works and saved it to show each other. It was... we laughed a lot when we saw that we'd found the same poem. An ocean apart."

Derek nodded. Sym let out a low rumble of a growl.

"She has power."

Charles glanced at the sea witch. "Yes, I've told you."

Sym shook her head. "There is something different. Wrong. May I?"

His insides twisted, but Charles handed over the scrap of paper. Sym took it with tender hands. She ran her fingers over both sides. She rubbed the ink, sniffed the paper, and even licked it.

Charles raised an eyebrow at Derek, who shrugged.

Sym sniffed the poem again, scrunched up her nose, and sneezed. She passed the parchment back to Charles with a grimace.

"Something is stifling her power. There are two distinct magical essences here. One is a faint trace I've smelled on you since we met, the other is something different. Older."

"The wizard," Charles said.

Sym nodded. "He might be older than me," she said with a look at Derek.

"What does that mean when it comes to getting Riva back?" Derek asked in a low voice.

"Any number of things," Sym murmured, her gaze going distant for a moment. They all watched her for a few seconds before Greggory scurried up her pants leg and onto her shoulder. He gave a tug on her earring, and she jerked. "It might mean he has much more power than me. It might mean he has lost much of his stamina. We can't know until we get there."

"How—" Derek began.

Britta shook her head and raised a hand. The four of them still stood by the hearth in the communal area of the inn. "This is not the place. Our largest room is available. You'll have more privacy there. I will do all I can to help you, though I—"

"You've done much." Charles put a hand on her shoulder. "We wouldn't ask any more of you."

She gave him a weak smile. "I tried to help her leave. I know she made it out the door. But something... something stopped her. She wouldn't tell me what."

"Magic." Sym picked a crumb of bread from the plate sitting abandoned at her seat and passed it up to the mouse on her shoulder. "Some kind of binding magic."

Charles winced, his insides aching at the thought of Riva bound to someone else, magically or not. "Let's get upstairs. I have questions for you, Sym. And I want to get an idea of what we are going to do when we face this wizard."

Chapter Sixteen

Silver Spoon

Riva and Lord Gadrel spent the night in separate rooms on the second floor of the Havita inn.

Around midnight, Riva rose from the bed, opened the door, and made her way quietly down the stairs. It would be foolish to try and leave again. Just the thought of it felt as though it drained her energy—though that might have been the lack of sleep.

She couldn't close her eyes without seeing either Charles's face furrowed in betrayal or her own covered with a wedding veil. Each time she'd fallen asleep that veil had suffocated her in her dreams.

So she sat by one of the two grand hearths in the inn's common room. She leaned against the stone, letting the warmth from the embers heat her back. Her fingers danced around the cuffs, fiddling with the fixings that kept them in her hair. If she tried it casually...

A shock slammed through her hands.

She cursed under her breath, hissing through clenched teeth and shaking out her arms as the tingling roved through her fingers and up to her wrists. The cuffs glowed, those symbols alight again.

The little shock wasn't enough to cause damage, but she wasn't getting rid of her chains anytime soon.

Riva wondered at Gadrel's claims of teaching her how to harness her magic. Surely he guessed that if she learned enough she'd find a way to break free. Or perhaps he was powerful enough to not worry. If that was the case, why take her in the first place?

She leaned her head against the wall, frustration rolling through every inch of her. Frustration and exhaustion. She hadn't felt so tired the night before, or even in the carriage as they'd rumbled over uneven roads for hours.

It reminded her of the few times she'd been ill as a child. As though her fever was raging, her mind rippling with unsteady thoughts, and her energy low enough to urge her to stay in bed all day.

If it weren't for the dreams.

Rustling sounded nearby, and Riva warily glanced toward it. A small woman moved toward her through the darkness. Riva recognized her from the square. She'd been one of the ones to linger, watching herself, Ian, and Gadrel.

"Hello," Riva said mildly.

The woman, who looked as though *girl* might be a more appropriate descriptor, halted in her tracks. Wide dark eyes met Riva's, just visible in the dim light.

"I..."

"It's all right." Riva waved a hand, gesturing for the girl to join her. "I couldn't sleep. The hearth is still warm. You're welcome to it."

The girl swallowed and scurried forward. Her movements were mouse-like. Nearly silent, as though she was used to being, or was required to be, as quiet as possible.

"I'm—"

"I know who you are," she interrupted Riva's attempt at an introduction. "You're the princess. The Lord's fiancée."

A low growl rumbled from Riva's throat before she clamped her lips closed. She inhaled and shook her head. "I'm Gadrel's captive, if anything. We are not engaged."

The girl watched her for a moment with those wide eyes, then broke into a soft chuckle. "That makes more sense. We were curious."

"We?" Riva's brow furrowed.

"The villagers," the girl said. "Talk's been going nonstop since the carriage pulled up. The Lord says a lot of things."

Riva tilted her head, but let silence fall in the hope that the girl would go on. She did.

"He said rain would come, but the crops are dry. He said he would stop taking life from the land, but even the village is becoming barren. He said he was bringing back a princess to save us all, but..."

"I'm not..." A sinking feeling weighed heavy on Riva's chest. "I'm not here to save anyone. I was brought here to marry him because of magic I can't control."

"You have magic?" The excitement in her voice broke Riva's heart a little.

She shook her head. "Not magic I have any control over. Sorry to disappoint."

"Oh. Is that what those are for?"

Riva followed the girl's pointing finger to the cuffs affixed to her hair. "How do you..."

"I recognize the markings. I clean the tower."

Riva shook her head again, eyebrows drawn together in confusion. "What tower?"

"The Lord's tower. I'm the maid."

Riva hesitated. "Forgive me, but if you're the maid for the tower, why are you here?"

The girl shrugged. "No one is allowed there while the Lord is gone. Even when he's there, I usually work short days in the winter. You can't go through the forest in the dark."

"So you have to leave here every morning?"

"And return before sunset, yes, Princess."

Riva sighed. "It's Riva. You can call me Riva."

The girl smiled. "I'm Sarah."

❧ ❦

Morning came with a red tinge on the horizon. They'd go to the tower today, a trek through the forest Riva was not looking forward to, given the fear most of the villagers shared about the place.

No one went in after dark, and though she'd heard a handful of warnings over breakfast, there had been a suspicious lack of specifics. Part of her wondered if the wizard had created tales of disappearances and attacks simply to keep people away from his tower when he was sleeping.

Riva straightened in her seat. She'd begun dozing again, nearly falling into her breakfast for the second time. She was even more drained now than she'd been the night before. A few hours' sleep was clearly not enough.

A tall, middle-aged woman with vibrant red hair and sapphire blue eyes planted a mug of tea beside Riva's plate. She'd introduced herself the night before as Tarissa. She owned and ran the inn they'd spent the night in. Riva recognized her as the one who had not bothered to hide her disdain for Gadrel when they'd arrived in Havita.

"His Lordship will be down soon. He ate in his rooms as usual," Tarissa told Riva.

Riva nodded and licked her chapped lips. "Thank you for the meal. I'm sorry to be so... well, so tired."

"It's not you." Tarissa reached across the table and patted Riva's wrist. "Be careful, you hear?"

Riva's brow furrowed, her mind muddled with a string of confusing thoughts that couldn't break the barrier of sleepy fog at the front of her head.

She opened her mouth to ask what the woman meant, but footsteps thudded down the wooden stairs, and she plopped a chunk of ham into her mouth instead.

"Princess." Lord Gadrel's voice sounded through the vast common room.

Riva scowled, but swallowed and turned to him, her voice emotionless. "Gadrel."

He gave a cocky smile and turned to Tarissa. "Have someone load my usual order onto the carriage. Sarah should meet us at the tower to prepare supper for the evening before she returns."

"Aye, Lord. She is already on her way."

A cold trickle sank through Riva's chest and settled in her stomach as he spoke. She studied his face, fury building as realization began to piece together like a puzzle.

Gadrel's skin was smooth. The grey in his hair was gone, replaced with the jet-black locks she'd seen that first day. His voice had regained the deep tone from before. Even his back was straighter.

Riva put a hand to her face. Her skin was chilly, a cold she hadn't been able to shake after leaving the fire the night before. Her hand moved, fingers crawling across her chest to the silver cuff hanging just past her shoulder.

Furious tears welled in her eyes.

Gadrel finished his instructions to Tarissa and waved a hand at Riva. "Finish quickly. We should be on our way soon."

She stood abruptly. The bench beneath her knocked back and thunked onto the ground.

Tarissa looked at her, eyes narrowed in a warning that Riva did not heed.

"You're stealing it."

Gadrel turned to her with an unbothered gaze.

The fury within her bubbled like a boiling pot. Riva's hands trembled at her sides, and she clenched them into fists. "These damned cuffs." She jerked at one and another spark of pain shot through her hand. She barely cared. "They're taking my magic, my power. And what? Feeding it to you?" Her face twisted in disgust.

Gadrel's easy stare flickered. He pursed his lips a moment, then flicked his hand at Tarissa.

The woman's mouth pinched into a straight line, but she gave a short bow before turning and calling to the few villagers scattered about eating. "Make your way outside. Your meals can continue shortly."

A few uttered the beginnings of complaints. But when they caught sight of Lord Gadrel standing at the head of Riva's table, they stood and quickly made their way out the back door of the inn.

Tarissa gave Riva one last look, a furrowed warning still in her brow. The door closed behind her.

"How dare you," Riva hissed through clenched teeth. She slammed her fist onto the table, anger roaring through her blood and chasing away the fatigue.

"How dare—"

"I'm not finished," she shouted. She swiped her hand across the table and sent her plate and cup smashing to the floor. "You claim to want to teach me, to want to marry me, and instead you siphon my power—"

"Power a girl like you has *no* right to," Gadrel spat.

Riva sucked in a breath at the dripping contempt in his voice. "Because I'm a woman?"

"Because you're a princess with no training, no control, and a silver spoon stuck between you and any chance at practicing *real* magic."

Riva took a few blind steps toward him, unsure of how to cause the most harm, but absolutely certain she'd rip his eyes out with her own fingers if that was what it took to free herself from this nightmare.

Gadrel put up a hand.

A reverberation went through the air. Visible, as though wind had been painted with shades of grey. Riva stopped in her tracks, not pulled back by the chains in her hair but held at a distance by the barrier Gadrel had created.

"You never planned to teach me." Her voice shook with fury. "You only ever wanted my power."

"Your power and your name," Gadrel corrected. His features smoothed as Riva ceased her attempts to get closer. He raised his chin. "You will marry me, Princess. And when you do, all will know of my might and power."

She snarled. "You mean *my* power."

He scoffed. "You do not know how to wield it. I do. That makes it mine."

Tears dripped down her cheeks, but there was no sadness within.

Gadrel sighed. "I tried to be kind, Riva. This life doesn't have to be a prison. I can still teach you as I promised."

"If I comply."

He inclined his head.

She bit out her words. "I will never marry you. My heart is with another. He *will* come find me."

"I doubt he even knows where you've gone."

Anger flashed like lightning across her face.

"I suggest you calm yourself, Princess. We leave shortly."

Riva watched him pause to pluck a piece of toast from a plate at the head of the table. He took a bite, brushed crumbs from his mustache, and then strode out the main door of the inn.

With trembling fingers, Riva picked up her dishes and stacked them in a neat pile. She righted the wooden bench and warmed her hands for a moment at the roaring fire in the hearth. The smell of fresh bread wafted through the room. A loaf was nearly done cooking in a small grate above the fireplace.

A silver spoon.

A royal name.

Magic she never asked for.

And a prince. Hopefully, a prince on his way to help her escape.

CHAPTER SEVENTEEN
The Great Cleanse

"What happened here?" Derek knelt at the edge of the river, running his fingers through the dusty, ruddy dirt. They'd had to stop at the river border between Faytrue and the Hidden Hamlet.

The horses had bucked at the bridge. Even Sym's sea beast resisted the crossing. It was Charles's gentle coaxing that had gotten them all to the other side.

They'd given the horses a chance to drink from the river on the Hamlet side, and Derek took the opportunity to survey the stark contrast.

Greggory, perched on Derek's knee, squeaked.

Derek looked at Sym for a translation.

"He doesn't like it," she said in a distracted voice, her gaze going past Derek and upriver. "Says he's with the horses on wanting to stay on the Faytrue side."

"What's wrong with the land, Sym?" Derek asked. "Where did the green go?"

She shook her head. With a slow turn, she looked at Charles. "The power your princess has... how strong is she?"

Derek glanced at his brother, a chill tightening his chest.

"She's strong," Charles said, pride in his tone. "Accidentally slammed me into a wall one time. I don't sneak up on her anymore." He laughed, but the sound died quickly.

"The wizard who took her." Sym wrinkled her nose. "His stench is everywhere. It coats these lands, as though his essence replaced every living thing as he drained the soil of its energy."

"Sym," Derek said carefully. "What do you mean he drained the soil?"

She met his gaze, then Charles'. "I should tell you on the way. I don't think we have time to squander."

<hr>

Derek found himself, yet again, acting as a mount for Greggory. The little mouse started in front of him on the saddle and had worked his way up to Derek's shoulder. Tiny claws held a chunk of his hair, jerking it on occasion when the horse kicked up or slowed unexpectedly.

Greggory squeaked.

"I know," Derek sighed, not able to understand, but pretty sure he got the gist of what the mouse was saying. "I'll get an earring like Sym's after all this is done. I don't like you having to hold my hair either."

The satisfied grunt from the little creature made Derek smile.

"Sym?" Charles prompted.

The three of them rode side by side with Sym in the middle. She nodded, her gaze distant and fixed ahead of them. Derek turned his attention to her as well.

The sea witch sucked in a breath, and Derek wondered for the first time since they'd been on this side of the river if something about the dry arid landscape was harming her in some way. It hadn't occurred to him, though the climate in the mountains had been a struggle for her, that this might be as difficult, if not more so.

He tilted his head, trying to catch a glimpse of the black cracks on her skin without being overt. Even from the distance required between horses, and her tangle of black hair loose in the wind, it was clear the cracks had grown.

A stirring of worry grew in his stomach as Sym began her explanation.

"Not everything has life. A rock, a long-dead fossil, the dirt beneath our feet. They have no heartbeat, no blood, no breath. They are not *alive*. But they do have power. There is an energy in our world that suffuses everything, warm and living, cold and stone, alike."

Charles nodded. "Cerulean has many legends about the power of the land, the trees, even some of the animals. Many think that power is what protects our island from the conflicts on the continent and the pirates who rove the oceans."

Sym inclined her head. "I'm certain that is part of it, though Cerulean itself has built a reputation to keep itself safe as well."

"So this place," Derek gestured, "has been drained of that energy?"

"Yes." Sym released the reins and rubbed her fingers together. Black cracks spread along her hands now as well, stemming from her cuticles and crawling nearly to her knuckles on some of them. "Listen close, Princes, for this is information long lost to your people. Indeed, to most of the humans in this world."

Derek inched his steed closer to hers. Greggory patted his cheek.

"There are many forms of magic," Sym began. "Some come from within. From your descriptions, that is where Riva's power stems. Other magic grows from the land. Mystical plants one might collect and use in potions and poultices. Magical creatures one might hunt or find and strike a bargain with. The ocean is a vast source of both."

She paused, then stretched her hand out and gestured at the nothingness around them. "The final source is the land itself. The world, and all the energy and power within each rock, pebble, grain of sand. That is the most difficult to harness, because if you pull the energy from a pebble, you have very little. If you pull it from a mountain, you have enough to perhaps devastate a kingdom."

Derek swallowed. He turned his gaze on the landscape. "Why, though?"

Sym sighed. "My guess, and it is a guess, is that he had power within himself. That is how most of us start. Eventually, likely after a hundred years or more of practicing magic, that power diminished as all things do. From there..."

"He stole it from the land to keep his power," Derek finished when Sym went quiet.

She nodded.

"And now," Charles spoke through clenched teeth, his knuckles white around the reins of his horse, "he wants to do the same to Riva."

"She was a well-kept secret," Sym murmured, just loud enough for them to hear. "Power of that kind is impossibly rare. The Great Cleanse four hundred years ago was the last uniting moment for every kingdom, and since then, magic users have been in hiding or gone extinct."

Derek shifted on his saddle, a rush of uncomfortable guilt heating his neck. His ancestors had been a part of the ruling elite who had executed the order to dash magic from the face of the world. Historical texts were unclear as to why such hatred and violence was perpetuated throughout the lands, and Cerulean had been much milder in their efforts during the Great Cleanse. But the fact remained that his bloodline had been responsible for a great loss.

"We have to get to her," Charles said. He heaved a breath and met his brother's eye.

Derek nodded. "And we have to be careful. If this wizard has been drawing energy from the land, who knows how powerful he has become?"

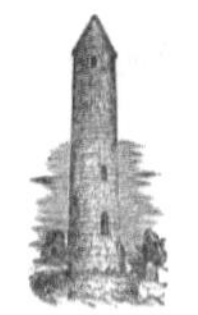

Chapter Eighteen

The Tower

The tower was beautiful. Old and cracked, ivy growing along the stone and dirty windows with rusty hinges, yet none of the flaws detracted from the immensity of the structure nor the awe it inspired.

The thing was nearly as tall as the parapets that rose over the Faytrue royal palace. A narrow balcony extended from a wide window at the very top. So high Riva had to crane her neck to make it out.

Forest surrounded them. Vast trees reached their branches in vain as they tried to attain the height of the tower. The largest of the great evergreens rose, perhaps, to the edge of the balcony, still over a dozen feet from the top of the pointed roof.

The trek through the forest had been peaceful. An odd contrast to the stories and warnings Riva had heard. She'd stuck to the window of the carriage, her focus anywhere but on the thief sitting across from her.

She now stood rigid before the wizard's home. Gadrel strode to the wide wooden doors at the base of the tower, his cloak billowing behind him. Sarah waited at the door and dipped into a low curtsey as he approached.

"Is the princess's room ready?"

The girl kept her gaze on the ground, and a fresh stirring of anger kicked into Riva's chest.

"Yes, my Lord. And supper has been started. It will be ready before nightfall."

"Good. I'd hate for you to return to Havita in the dark."

Sarah's cheeks went pale. She straightened with a nod and then pulled open one of the double doors.

Gadrel walked in without a glance at Riva.

Sarah caught Riva's eye, gave an urgent 'come on' gesture, and danced on her toes until Riva sighed and followed Gadrel through the door.

❦

They dined together before the sun set. Riva's plans required soothing Gadrel's pride and temper, so when the bell rang in her room to call her to dinner, she obediently followed the winding stairs down to the dining room.

The tower was slim. Most floors were single rooms. The kitchen was at the bottom, the dining room one floor up, and a series of studies, libraries, and Gadrel's rooms took the middle floors. Riva's room was a sprawling thing at the very top with only the balcony window for natural light.

Riva ran her fingers across the thick rectangles of carved stone as she trudged down the steps. Slitted windows allowed smoke from the sconces in the stairwell to escape but did little to allow in light. Not that it mattered; darkness was falling quickly outside. Cold came with the approaching night.

She reached the dining room and pushed open the wooden door. Gadrel waited within, standing before a circular table laid out with a feast of meats, cheeses, rolls, roasted vegetables, a creamy soup of some kind, and a plateful of baked desserts. Sarah gave a short curtsey as Riva entered the room and then scurried away to the kitchen. The faint sounds of scrubbing dishes echoed up from the stairwell.

"Does Sarah cook like this every day?" Riva asked.

Gadrel cast her a mild smile. "No, this is to celebrate your arrival."

Riva swallowed down her grimace and nodded. "I will have to thank her."

"Of course." Gadrel pulled out a chair, motioning for her to sit.

She did, her mind torn between keeping up a charade of peace and her plans for later that night. Outside, the sun began to paint the horizon orange and pink.

They shared trivial conversation. Gadrel enjoyed talking more and more as Sarah refilled his wine, so Riva let him. He told her of his past: building the tower in his youth, adventuring in the surrounding forests before the village was formed, taking refuge there during the Great Cleanse, and eventually allowing settlers fleeing war to build their village with the promise that they would serve him with dedication.

He revealed much, and Riva locked away little tidbits in her mind. His age was a surprise. As much as she expected him to be far older than he appeared, the fact that he'd been alive during the Cleanse meant he was several centuries older than she'd thought.

As the sun hit the tips of the trees, Sarah returned to pour one last goblet of wine. "My Lord, nightfall approaches. May I—"

"Yes, yes." He waved a dismissive hand. "Hurry on home. Return early in the morning. You'll have this to clean up."

Riva's jaw clenched, but she remained quiet, giving Sarah a tight smile as the girl hurried from the room.

"Will she get home in time?" Riva asked, working to keep her voice mild.

Gadrel shrugged. "I assume so. She's left this late before when there was work to be done."

Riva inhaled and swallowed down her next words. Instead, she fell quiet again and allowed him to consume the conversation once more. It wasn't long, however, before he mentioned the wedding, and she excused herself to bed. He gave no resistance and did not appear to notice when she pocketed a small butter knife from the breadboard.

His mannerisms at dinner surprised her. She imagined some of his ease came from being home and thinking he'd finally won her submission. Perhaps he figured she had nowhere to go if she managed to get away now. Maybe he thought the villagers would refuse to help her for fear of angering him. Maybe he knew she wouldn't act rashly while Sarah was there for fear of him hurting the girl.

Riva's legs ached by the time she reached her room. She collapsed onto the bed, staring up at the slanted ceiling above. Benji would enjoy this room. He'd beg her to hang ropes from the beams. He'd stack the furniture, scramble up the walls, and create a perch from which to watch everything.

Her heart ached. Her position in the kitchen had to have been replaced by now. Marian needed an extra set of hands helping.

That guard by the gate was probably glad she was gone.

She ran a hand down her hair to one of the cuffs. Matching engravings marked much of the stone tower. Protection runes.

She didn't need protection.

Riva sat up, her hand slipping under the pillow at the head of the bed. She'd never needed anyone's protection. She'd only ever needed and wanted friends. And, with all her oddities, with her bloodline and hair and power, she'd always had them. People who cared for her. Not because she was a princess, but because she'd shown that she cared for them.

Befriending good people had always come easy.

Her fingers found a thin piece of metal, and she pulled it forth. It had only been an hour after she'd settled in her room when there had been a soft knock at the door.

"I can't get you any sort of key," Sarah whispered, fear glinting in her wide eyes.

"Do nothing," Riva replied. She shook her head. "Do nothing that may get you in trouble with the wizard, Sarah. I will make my own way."

The girl shook her head. "I couldn't get a key. But I got you this."

Riva eyed the stamp in her hand. A small metal tool used to mark runes into lesser metals. Twine was looped around the handle end, a slip of paper labeling it as a *Dispel Rune*.

CHAPTER NINETEEN

This I Vow

The butter knife glowed with the dispel rune. She'd stamped both sides and now held the hair cuff firmly in one hand, forcing the edge of the dull blade against the clasp mechanism with the other.

The magic in the cuff understood her intention. The runes flared, searing her hand. She sucked a breath through clenched teeth. The pain grew and she considered stopping, letting the cuff remain, trying again another time...

Though oceans stretch between us now

I'll see you again, this I vow

The words from the poem, words she'd whispered in Charles's ear before each parting, echoed in her mind. She sucked in a breath and whispered them aloud.

The cuff popped.

The searing suddenly ceased, and she released the silver with a gasp. It fell to the bed, no longer glowing. Rather, it was resting, innocent and plain, on the thick blanket.

Riva looked at her hand. Her fingers burned with pain, blisters forming on several while red chapped skin marred her palm.

She'd have to switch hands for the remaining cuff. Which would mean handing the butter knife with her aching, ruined hand. She thought about asking her power to heal her again.

Weariness dragged at her bones at the very notion. It was impossible to know how much Gadrel had taken from her, but she knew she had not yet recovered.

A stir of unease rolled through her stomach. Would she have the strength to flee that night? Or would she be forced to wait until morning? How long would it take for Gadrel to notice the cuffs were no longer fixed in her hair?

How long would it take for her power to return? And when it did, would she be able to control it enough to defend herself?

Riva closed her eyes and pressed her uninjured palm against her forehead. An ache grew behind her eyes, thundering at her temples and threatening to overcome her senses.

The desire to sleep was so strong.

Riva?

She jolted, the voice so familiar and welcome that tears sprang to her eyes. She glanced around, searching every shadow in the room as she murmured, "Charles?"

This is so strange. Listen, I don't have long. I love you. I'm coming, Riva. I'm coming. Don't—

The sound cut out as though he'd suddenly stopped speaking.

Riva sucked in a breath, the tears in her eyes falling at the rush of relief that flooded her system. Her hand trembled, and she exhaled through pursed lips.

If Charles was coming, and she had no desire to believe otherwise, she needed to be ready to run.

No. She needed to be ready to protect him. Charles had his heart, but no magic beyond his unending capacity to love.

She wrapped a cloth around her injured hand and another around the remaining cuff. With a grimace and a pull from the well of anger within her, she grasped the silver and used the stamped butter knife to remove it as well.

The runes flared, heating past the point of discomfort. She released the cloth when it began smoking, biting through the pain now roaring in both hands until—

It was gone. The cuff fell. Rolled off the bed and clunked onto the rug laid over the stone floor.

Riva's hair cascaded at her sides. The golden strands pooled on the bed, knotted and tangled in places from having to sleep with it in the cuffs.

She ran her blistered fingers through her hair with a wince. The strength she so often felt there, the power that hummed within her, was a muted murmur now.

Still, whatever part of her magic that remained must have felt her hurt. Maybe found camaraderie with her after being jailed so long. Maybe knew she had been the one to release it.

Her hair sputtered with light. The glow focused around her hands and the fingers still brushing through the strands.

It eased the pain. The blisters shrank, the sharp red faded to pink, and within minutes she was able to clench her fists normally.

Riva inhaled, clutching the memory of Charles's voice to her heart. Then she stood and darted to the balcony window.

Evening was settling in. The light quickly faded but was not yet gone.

A winding section of tied-together sheets sat in a bundle on the balcony. She'd done the work before dinner in case removing the cuffs truly destroyed her ability to do simple things like tying knots.

Riva didn't know how long the sheets would reach. The likelihood that they extended to the bottom of the tower was low. It didn't matter. She'd jump the rest of the way if she had to.

Her hands shook as she yanked at the sheet. It was secure. She'd fastened it to one of the pillars on either side of the balcony holding up a shallow awning that protected it from rain.

Jitters danced through her stomach. She tossed the bulk of the fabric over the edge of the short stone rail. A glance over the edge showed the sheet dangling above the ground, though how far above the dirt it hung was nearly impossible to tell from so high up.

She gripped the tied off end with her right hand, settled her butt against the sheets, and looped them around her left hand. She planted her feet against the stone edge of the balcony and pushed off.

The momentum carried her further from the tower than she'd planned. A rush of fear slammed through her. Sweat beaded on her brow, her heart raced, and she barely glanced down before forcing herself to look at the stone wall ahead of her. The sheet swung back toward the tower, and Riva used the movement to plant her feet firmly on the stone.

Arms aching, breath hissing through clenched teeth, she slowly lowered herself down.

Seconds ticked by. Minutes melted together. Time seemed to stretch as the stars appeared overhead, the sunlight still just bright enough to help guide her way.

Riva stopped every now and then to shake out one hand, then the other. Her hair, braided into three segments which were in turn braided together into one, felt heavy on her back.

After what felt like an hour but was likely closer to a few minutes, she glanced down. The ground was maybe twenty feet away.

The end of the sheet was perhaps five.

Riva grimaced. But she'd known it was coming. Hoped her plan would have put her nearer to safety but hadn't counted on it.

She hugged the wall the rest of the way down, reached the end of the fabric, gritted her teeth, and jumped.

A sickening crack accompanied the twist as her left foot hit the ground first. A yelp of pain escaped her clenched jaw.

She staggered up, dusting the dirt from her arm, and glancing around with wide eyes. It was darker here. The great evergreens blocked the remaining glow of sunlight on the horizon and left her in chilling shadow.

She limped a few paces. A deep desire within her demanded she put distance between herself and the tower. However, as she reached the edge of the woods, a familiar voice called out.

"You've learned nothing."

Riva whirled. She put her weight on her right foot, hands balled into fists.

Gadrel strode toward her, his long cloak billowing in the night. "I magicked those cuffs, Princess. How could you think I wouldn't notice when they stopped feeding me your power?"

Riva swallowed. "I'd hoped you were asleep after all that wine."

"I don't need to sleep," Gadrel said. "Not with the power you're supplying."

"I'm not. Not anymore."

He scowled. "Indeed. I underestimated you. Not many would be able to remove them. That was powerful magic."

A low growl rumbled in her throat. "Not magic. Sweat and pain and determination, Gadrel. That's what gets things done. Not *magic*."

He stopped a few feet from her, just at the edge of the tree line. His dark eyes studied her for a long moment. "I wish I didn't need you, Riva. But all things run out of time eventually. Between you and me, I'd prefer to hold on a while longer. Even if it means you do not."

Riva's throat went dry. "Given up on marriage, then?"

Gadrel shook his head. "We will be wed. You'll survive long enough for your name to give me all the credence I need to expand the Hamlet into a real kingdom. By the time I've drained you of every ounce of power in your bones, it will be too late for anyone to stop me."

"You won't get the chance for all that," Riva whispered. If she spoke too loudly the fear threatening to bring her to her knees would be heard in her voice. "My love is coming. He will help me escape you, and when I do, I will make sure the surrounding kingdoms are warned of your ill intent."

"Hmm." Gadrel cocked his head, a thoughtful frown replacing the smug expression he usually wore. "Your love, you say?"

Riva nodded. Her nostrils flared, the memory of Charles's voice ringing through her ears.

A smile split Gadrel's lips, and Riva's blood went cold with dread.

"Let's give him an invitation, then."

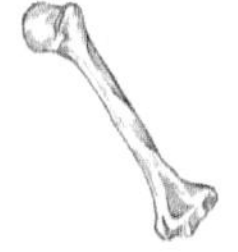

Chapter Twenty

Message in a Bone

Charles clenched his fist around the bone fragment, eyes welling with tears as he raised his head to meet Sym's gaze.

"It was her," he choked out. "I heard her voice."

The sea witch gave a solemn nod. "We are close now, Prince. I'll take that back."

He handed over the bone.

They stood outside, behind a fairly large inn at the center of Havita. The dry, dead land had shifted when they'd reached the town, but the mood had not. Villagers had watched them pass with wide, sunken eyes. And, though a forest rose up not far in the distance, even in the town it felt as though everything was muted and dull.

The sun had begun to set. As it fell to the horizon, Charles's anxiety grew. They needed to be on their way. Yet Derek had spoken to the villagers. He'd talked to the woman who ran the inn. He'd learned troubling rumors about the forest at night.

When his brother had declared they would leave for the tower in the morning, Charles had balked.

Mid-way into a good shouting match, Sym had taken him aside. Charles followed her begrudgingly. She hadn't explained much, only told him that he might be able to speak to Riva. They were close now, and though her magic was dimmed in this arid place, Sym had enough power to let him reach his beloved.

The spell had been so quick. He'd heard her say his name, but had Riva heard him tell her to stay there? Had she heard him say they were coming at first light?

"You've done all you can in this moment," Sym murmured.

Charles nodded. His gaze was fixed on the trees. He had no doubt there were dangerous beasts lurking within. He'd seen his share of haunted forests. The little hairs on the back of his neck stood on end just being so close to the dense trees.

"First light." He said it quietly. Almost a question, perhaps more a confirmation.

Sym met his eye. "First light. This wizard... he has broken many of the ancient oaths those of us alive before the Great Cleanse promised to keep." She shook her head. The cracks on her skin seemed darker, more sunken in the fading evening light. "Equal trades, Charles. Magic is supposed to give as much as it takes."

He let out a soft sigh, his chest tight with worry. "Have you always abided by those rules?"

The corner of her mouth twitched. "Yes. Though one with a shorter lifespan might not see the larger picture. Those who come away displeased with their deals are often dead before it is finished being painted."

His brow furrowed. "Derek mentioned our family. Generations ago?"

She nodded. "They were displeased. And yet, their descendants flourish. Your mother's changes have started Cerulean on a path to such enlightenment and revolution as the world has not seen in ages. Since before *my* time."

"And you made that happen?" Charles was too tired and worried to keep the skepticism out of his voice.

She chuckled. "No. I didn't *make* anything happen. But magical bargains forged in the past do have a bearing on the future. You have a different view of the world than your brother, for all his blessings and graces. You will not forget the second sons. You will not forget the children of Cerulean when they fall into your care."

"Derek wouldn't forget them."

Sym's smile grew. "Your loyalty is admirable, Prince. I am merely stating that they will thrive under a different level of attention with you as king."

Charles swallowed.

He knew it was coming. Had known since the weight of the crown pressed against his dark hair. Since the portrait of his family that hung in the palace hall had changed. Yet hearing that he would someday be king from the lips of a sea witch who was at least four-hundred years old sent a different kind of shock through him.

"We should return indoors," Sym said, her head tilted slightly, studying him as though she was reading his every thought. "I sense things stirring in the woods."

They returned to the inn.

Sym headed to the fire, warming her long fingers a little too close to the blazing heat.

Charles sought out his brother.

Derek sat hunched over a bowl of stew in a far corner. A dagger rested on the table an inch from his free hand. His bright blue eyes followed Charles from the door, assessing the room for any threats as his brother joined him at the table.

"I thought you trusted these people," Charles murmured as he sank into a seat across from Derek.

"I believe them about the forest," Derek replied, his voice equally low. "That doesn't mean I trust them."

Footsteps thudded across the stone behind Charles, and he glanced up, leaning back to make room for his own bowl of stew as the redheaded innkeeper placed it on the table before him.

To his surprise, she didn't leave. Instead, the woman shifted her skirts and settled at the end of the table between him and Derek.

"Why are you here? Really?"

Derek let his spoon rest against the side of the bowl and leaned back. He plucked the dagger from the table, running his fingers over the engraved handle with an even expression. "Why do you want to know?"

Heat flushed Charles's face. He watched the woman carefully. Her eyes flashed at the challenge in Derek's tone.

She pursed her lips and heaved a sigh. "We've been under the thumb of Lord Gadrel for generations. Our ancestors settled here with the promise of protection, and freedom from the kingdoms who despised us." She shook her head, locks of red hair cascading to her shoulders, and gestured out at the common room of her inn. "This is what we want. Simple lives. And that was well and good for a time. But as the years passed, the Lord's magic began to fade. And as his power shrank, his cruelty grew."

Charles caught Derek's eye at this, fresh fear flashing through his chest. "We know he's been draining the land of its innate power."

She nodded. "The forest was not always a dangerous place. But the dark creatures of the Hamlet could not survive what it became. They moved closer to the tower to avoid the fate of lesser beings."

"What are they?" Derek asked in a low voice. "These dangerous things in the forest? Because my brother and I are no strangers to fighting monsters."

The woman bowed her head. "The same words were spoken by many of our people years ago. When they first began arriving. You might kill a few. You might make it to the tower before they overcome you. But we've lost so many..."

Her eyes glistened with tears, hands clenching on the tabletop.

Charles swallowed. "We don't mean to bring up this pain lightly. But I *have* to get to Riva."

"I understand. Lord Gadrel has caused enough suffering. I know you're only here for your princess, but if you were able to defeat him..."

"We are here to right a wrong."

Charles glanced over his shoulder. Sym stood behind him with her chin high and a blazing look in her eyes.

The others looked at her as well, and she continued, "But it seems we are now to right several."

She met Derek's eyes, and the prince nodded. A slow smile grew across Sym's face. "It's sort of what we do."

CHAPTER TWENTY-ONE
Fear and Fury

R iva screamed. Not a cry of agony, but a wretched sound of fear and fury.

She stood on the balcony, tears streaming down her cheeks as the many days of holding everything in finally broke. A dam of emotion flaring out of her with no method nor desire to control it.

Her hair spiraled in the air as though filled with static. The wind tugged at its ends, pulling the strands over the edge of the stone parapet and out to float amongst the arcs of gold light it created.

The power was trapped. Held in a bubble of force Gadrel had formed around the balcony when he'd used his magic to get her back to the top of the tower.

Blood was crusted under her nails from the effort she undertook to fight being restrained. If her power had been stronger... if he hadn't been feeding on it for days...

The forest below was dark. Not the nightly shade of black that might have been unsettling but at least would have been familiar. No, this was an unnatural lack of light. Lord Gadrel stood at the edge of the trees, dark grey mist emanating from his palms as he murmured an incantation.

Riva didn't know what the mist would do. She didn't know if it would dissipate by the time Charles reached the edge of the woods. She didn't know if he was already there, perhaps amongst the trees already. Perhaps overcome with this evil darkness that might swallow him whole.

She screamed through the incantation. Shouted and railed as Gadrel turned from the forest and strode to the tower door. A vicious spike of satisfaction quieted her for a brief moment at the sight of his marred face.

Scratches ran down his cheek, bruises forming across his eye socket from where she'd struck him before he'd managed to get his magic between them. He'd aged as well. The choice to use his power for whatever dark magic now encompassed the forest meant he would have to steal from her again before he returned to his youthful graces.

It wouldn't be tonight.

Not after how hard he'd struggled to get her back in the tower room. Not after the drain he'd put on himself for his wicked *invitation* to her prince.

Riva's chest heaved as her shouting finally faded, her emotions spent. Her hair drifted down, cascading around her and to the floor. The sun was gone now.

What would morning bring?

She turned from the balcony. Candles lit the room, but the air was as frigid as it was outside. She closed the windows and secured the latch. Her mind flickered through plans and ideas, desperate hopes and crushing realizations.

Memories surfaced. Days when her power had flared enough to leave her feeling almost as drained as she was now. A good rest—that had always helped. A good rest and some of Marian's savory pies.

She needed to be strong.

Riva strode to a small table laden with non-perishable snacks. She took her time, going back and forth between eating and plaiting her hair.

When both were done, she heaved the dresser in front of the door, crawled into bed, and attempted to will herself to sleep. Rest and strength. That was what she needed now. That was what would save her.

She dreamt of Charles. Shining, sun-filled days on the outskirts of the city, lazing on low-hanging branches, laying out in flowering fields. His dark hair curling around her fingers, those eyes looking at her as nothing and no one ever had.

The second son. A man who did not desire her for status. A man who believed in magic, in the fairy tales his mother had told him as a child. A man who was neither afraid of her power nor wanted to control it.

They'd shared so many dreams, for their future together and the future of their kingdoms.

She clung to those dreams. Let them fuel her recovery through the night even as her heart ached and shadows clung to the corners of her tower room.

CHAPTER TWENTY-TWO

Righting Wrongs

Derek met Sym's eye with a nod and a rueful grin. She'd come a long way from making deals in a dark ocean cave. And she was correct; righting wrongs did seem to be a habit they'd fallen into.

From the first town they'd stopped at all those weeks ago, they'd found problems all across the kingdom. Small things they could help with, and sometimes not so small. They'd made friends along the way, picked up new skills, and aided many people.

Fighting a centuries-old wizard felt like a different sort of challenge. One that was far more likely to get them killed than stealing a goose.

A bit of him cringed at the thought. These people—he glanced around the inn at the flocks of villagers who had come in for a warm meal and company—were regular folks. Innocents trying to live peaceful lives. And the wizard had stolen that from them, the same way he'd stolen Riva.

Derek's thoughts turned to Alyana. Though they'd only spent a few days together on their mission to rescue Lady Lydia, their friendship was one that Derek knew would stretch for many years. He missed her snarky comments and the constant reminders that life was not the same for a peasant as it was for a prince.

Sym offered perspective, but an incredibly powerful sea witch's perspective. It wasn't quite the same.

Derek rose from his seat, drawing the eye of his brother. He raised a hand to keep Charles where he sat and crossed the room to where the innkeeper chatted with an elderly couple as she passed them bowls of the evening stew. He waiting until she turned to him before addressing her.

"What was your name, madam?"

"Tarissa."

He nodded. "Tarissa, would you be able to give me some details of the tower? Perhaps a map of the forest in this area?"

She wiped her hands on her apron, then took his shoulder and steered him away from the table. "Sarah would be the one to help with that. She works as a maid for Lord Gadrel."

"Where can I find her?"

Tarissa paused, and her face fell. Lips barely parted, she darted away from him toward the front of the inn. She scanned the front counter before whirling and looking out across the crowd.

Derek stepped toward her cautiously. "Madam?"

"She should have been back by now," Tarissa murmured, fingers pressed to her lips as she hurried past him toward the swinging door to the kitchen.

She returned before he had time to follow her, fear wild in her eyes. "I have to go check her house. She always comes here first, but—"

Her words were swallowed by a shout from outside.

Derek moved between Tarissa and the door, drawing his sword. She put a hand on his shoulder.

"That sounded like the miller."

"The town is safe?" Derek asked in a low murmur as the eyes of the patrons turned to the door as well.

She nodded.

Charles appeared at his side, blade drawn as well. "What's going on?"

Derek opened his mouth at the same time that the front door of the inn flew open.

A gust of cold night air swept across them all, but it wasn't the chill that sent a shiver down Derek's spine.

A tall man—he must have been the miller—moved into the inn. Beside him, clutching his arm as though it were the final floating plank of wood after a ship was downed in a storm, was a woman with dark hair and stark white eyes.

She was young, maybe sixteen, and wore simple clothes with a dirty apron over her skirts.

"Sarah?" Tarissa breathed. She moved forward, and the girl jerked away from the sound of her footsteps.

Derek inhaled, tightening his grip on his hilt for a moment before sliding the blade back in its sheath.

"I don't..." Sarah's voice was ragged, her breathing short and shallow. "Miss, I can't... I can't see."

Derek looked to Tarissa, who had hands on either side of the girl's face, staring into her wide, white eyes.

"This is the wizard's maid?"

Tarissa nodded. She straightened and removed her hands, wiping tears from her own face. "Thank you, Jacobs," she said to the miller. "I'll take her from here."

The tall man looked uneasy. "There's a mist creeping in. It's at the edge of the forest. Like it's waiting for something."

Derek glanced around for Sym.

The witch was close, standing incredibly still in a shadowed corner, her dark eyes taking in everything before her. She met his gaze and gave a shallow nod.

"It was him," Sarah said.

Everyone turned to her.

"The wizard?" Charles asked, his voice tight.

Sarah nodded. "I heard him. Heard his voice." She sniffed, wiping her nose with the back of her sleeve and reaching out. Tarissa took her hand, clutching tight. "I thought I was going to make it," she whimpered. "I was almost back, the sun wasn't down yet, Miss. But there was a fog. It came from behind me and there was... there was a voice... his voice... came with it."

Derek spoke softly, aware that his voice would be strange to her. He didn't want to scare her. "What did he say, Sarah?"

She flinched, her knuckles going white she held so tightly to Tarissa. "He was saying to come find her. He was telling someone I don't know, a man named Charles. He kept saying, 'Charles, come find her. Before it's too late.'"

Derek whirled at the same moment that Charles bolted for the door.

With a set of words that would have thoroughly infuriated his mother, Derek dashed after him into the night.

⁂

Charles had always been quick. But where Derek was long and angular, Charles was stocky and strong. Even in the dim light granted to them by the moon and the scattered torches in the town square, Charles was easy to find and easy to catch up with.

Derek picked up his pace, darting in front of Charles and blocking his path.

"Get out of my way, brother," Charles snarled.

Derek took half a step back. "I can't do that. You heard what Tarissa said. There are dark things in that forest. We don't stand a chance getting through it at night."

"*You* heard what the girl said," Charles snapped. "That bastard has Riva. He knows I'm coming. We have no idea what is happening in that tower while we sit and wait for the bloody sun." He gestured angrily at the trees not far in the distance. He tried to push past again and met Derek's hand planted firmly on his chest.

Derek clenched his jaw. An internal war raged. Every part of him wanted to keep his brother and Sym safe. Yet he knew Charles was right. Knew that Riva was not safer because she was being kept by a wizard rather than a warlord.

"Get out of my—"

"All right," Derek growled.

Charles met his gaze, brow furrowed with worry and confusion glinting in his eyes. "What?"

"You're right," Derek said. "She's not safe, and we don't have enough information to think we can wait until morning. Still, little brother, don't go off into the woods half-strung. Let's go back to the inn and get what knowledge we can from the girl. Let's find out everything possible before we go in there."

Charles hesitated, his gaze drifting to the forest again.

"Ten minutes," Derek murmured. He took hold of Charles's shoulder and held his gaze. "Ten minutes, then we go after her."

Charles swallowed. He nodded.

"Besides." Derek tried for a smile, but churning worry in his stomach dampened the effort. "We won't make it a dozen paces without Sym."

Charles did not laugh, but he also didn't sprint into the trees alone. He turned and strode toward the inn without another word.

Derek followed, the worry growing as his peripheral vision caught sight of movement just beyond the tree line.

CHAPTER TWENTY-THREE

Splinters in the Dark

Moonlight shot like splinters through the scraggly branches of the trees around them. The trail had started clear, a direct line through the forest to the tower. It hadn't taken long for the path to be lost in the darkness.

"The mist is odd," Sym murmured. She reached out, plucking Charles's sleeve.

He stepped closer, returning to her side. She'd pulled both princes back to her a few times already.

"Magic," Charles agreed. He blinked a few times, rubbing his eyes. "Is the spell you cast enough to keep the blindness at bay?"

Sym's face was shadowed in darkness, but he caught the movement of her nod. "It should, but I am not certain what kind of spell the wizard used. As I said before, waiting until dawn would have been the wise choice."

Derek spoke before Charles had the chance. "We don't have time, Sym. The call for Charles was clearly bait, but we can't afford to wait out the trap."

Charles murmured his thanks.

Sym heaved a sigh.

They'd only been in the forest for a few minutes. Charles tightened his grip on the hilt of his sword. A pouch of herbs hung at his belt—Sym had insisted they all take a share in case they got separated.

The innkeeper had given them all bundles of food and water. She'd also nearly begged them to wait until dawn.

Heat stirred in Charles's chest and belly. He *had* to reach Riva. A pull at his core told him so, insisted that he move toward her with all haste. Yet preemptive guilt gnawed at his insides. If something happened to Sym, to his brother...

He blinked again, using his free hand to rub his eyes. It was hard to tell with the encompassing darkness, but the edges of his vision seemed blurred.

"Are you two having any trouble seeing?" he whispered.

Silence followed his words.

Charles turned to his companions and found thick trunks and shadowed forest instead. He swallowed, then raised his voice.

"Sym? Derek?"

He stood still. Silent. Listening with all his might.

"*Here,*" came a distant call. It was ahead, to his left.

He darted toward the voice.

Charles stepped around a knotted cluster of trees and caught sight of Derek and Sym to the left of him. Just as he caught sight of the thing looming behind them.

The beast towered on hind legs but was cat-like in the shape of its head and limbs. Jet black with white streaks that no doubt kept it well hidden within the moon-light-streaked forest.

Derek and Sym were only a dozen yards away, searching the darkness for Charles. The creature took a step toward their exposed backs. Charles's blood went cold at the size of it, nearly half again as tall as his brother.

Time seemed to slow.

Derek called out again. "Charles?"

"*Behind you, brother,*" Charles shouted. He took a few steps, pulling his sword, then broke into a run as the creature raised a massive paw, claws glinting in the light.

Its yellow gaze flashed to him at the last second. Charles swung.

The creature made contact, and Derek yowled with pain as blood spurted from his arm.

He spun away, slashing wildly with his blade to distance himself from the cat-like thing.

Charles did not leave room for distance. He attacked.

The creature leaped back, attempting to angle around the sharp point of Charles's sword. He stayed on it, blade nicking and slicing. Droplets of foul-smelling blood made the mulch of the forest floor slick.

Sym hissed at the periphery of Charles's attention. He could no longer see her, though it didn't sound as though she were behind him.

The adrenaline of the fight had caused his vision to blur at the edges even more.

Mist swirled at his feet as he spun, slashing again. He missed. The creature took the opening to land a kick on Charles's chest.

It slammed him backward. His body cracked into a tree, and he slumped to the ground, all the air gone from his lungs.

Charles shook out of the stun and inhaled through his nose. The breath didn't quite fill his lungs. He tried again, wincing at the pain of expanding his chest with air.

Ahead of him, Derek had taken the lead. His sword flashed silver in the moonlight as he moved around the creature. It was surprisingly agile for its size and avoided many of Derek's attempts to strike it down.

"Almost..." Sym murmured from the far side of the fight. Her voice carried, low and gravely, not the usual sing-song tone Charles had grown used to.

He swallowed and clambered to his feet, leaning hard on the tree to keep himself standing. His ribs were damaged; pain stabbed through him with every breath.

His brother darted backward, barely dodging a direct kick from the thing. It grazed him. Derek let out another grunt of pain.

Charles leapt forward. He stood directly in front of the creature, the only way to fully see it now. The blurred darkness had grown, shallowing his vision by half.

His sword came down across the thigh of the beast, and he cringed at how quickly it found bone.

"Derek," the sea witch said again, that same distorted voice a distraction as Charles ducked low to miss a swinging claw.

"Charles," Derek shouted.

He couldn't turn. Couldn't look at Derek while keeping his dwindling vision on the creature.

A rushing sound and the scent of sea salt filled the air. Charles attempted to suck in a breath, but it was like he'd been kicked in the chest again. The oxygen was not enough.

Before him, the creature staggered.

Charles bent, the sword falling from his fingers as he struggled to inhale.

A body collided with him. Strong arms and a wiry frame shunted him several feet before he fell to the ground. His shoulder hit with force, eliciting a grunt of pain.

He blinked rapidly, fear flooding him as he searched for his attacker. The moonlight was gone. The stars overhead had disappeared.

He blinked again.

There was no difference in sight when he opened his eyes. Everything had gone dark.

CHAPTER TWENTY-FOUR

Nearly There

Derek winced as Charles's weight crushed his ankle. He'd managed to shove his brother out of range of Sym's spell, but the two had gone crashing to the ground as a result.

He watched, barely able to see through the thickening mist and darkness of the night, as the cat-like creature who had attacked them succumbed to Sym's magic.

The air caught a scent of sea salt, brine, and rotten fish. The creature clawed at its throat for breath. In its distraction, Sym stepped up behind it. She was shorter by more than a foot, but her blade found purchase. The point sank through the creature's back, the tip coming out the front of its bare, furry chest.

It sank to its knees and fell forward with a loud thud.

Silence surrounded them for a few precious seconds. Derek laid atop his brother, his leg twisted underneath them both, breathing fast.

Then Charles spoke.

"Derek?"

"Here, sorry," Derek grunted. He detangled himself from Charles and clambered to his feet. Another wince split his features as he tried to put weight on his foot.

"I can't..." Charles swallowed, and Derek knelt with every ounce of brotherly concern shooting through him. Charles sat with an arm rested on his knee, the other hand pushing sweaty hair back from his face. He rubbed his eyes with his fingers. "I can't see."

Derek cursed.

This was neither the time, nor the place, for him to have an injured ankle and Charles to be blind.

He glanced toward Sym. She'd pulled her blade from the cat-like creature's body and was cleaning it on a spare cloth drawn from her bag. She met his gaze, sheathed the blade, and strode toward him. Greggory let out a squeak from her shoulder.

"What is it?" she demanded.

Derek gestured to Charles, his lips pinched tight to keep from admonishing his brother for bringing them into this damned forest in the first place.

"I can't see," Charles said again, his voice a low murmur.

Sym reached up. Charles flinched as her fingers found him but settled after a second. She ran her hands across his face, pausing with her fingertips gently pressed to his eyelids.

Derek straightened, rolling his foot and grimacing at the pain such a motion produced. He'd slow them down. When they got moving again.

"My spell did nothing."

Derek glanced at Sym, noting the tension in her voice. "What?"

"My magic to keep the mist at bay. It did nothing."

"For Charles," Derek corrected. "We can still see, so it protected us."

She shook her head, black locks dancing around her shoulders as Greggory scurried down her arm and onto Charles's less excited body. The little mouse squeaked, gesturing to its eyes.

"Greggory, too." Derek nodded.

"No, Derek. My magic did nothing to protect us. Whatever spell is embedded in the mist only affected Charles."

"And the girl," Charles said. "The maid from the tower."

Derek frowned. "Why?"

Sym clasped Charles's hand and rose, guiding him to his feet. "I don't know. But we shouldn't stay here. The blood will attract other things."

Derek sighed, his jaw jutted to the side in frustration.

"I'm sorry," Charles muttered.

Derek closed his eyes. Then he clasped a hand onto his brother's shoulder. "This isn't your fault alone. I agreed that we shouldn't wait. Besides, Sym and I can see, and if this is spellwork then it can be reversed. Right, Sym?"

She made a noncommittal noise.

Derek glared.

"I shouldn't have let you come with me," Charles said.

Derek scoffed. "As though I'd let you go alone. Come on. We should move." He gripped Charles's arm to guide him and glanced at Sym. "Which way?"

She looked at the sky and tilted her head. A few seconds later she pointed a long, sharp fingernail into the woods.

Derek inhaled. "Where would we be without you, Sym?"

She moved ahead of him to lead the way through the trees.

"You'd be crown prince," she muttered. "And probably rc-cngaged to a new, not-drowned princess."

Derek cringed and followed her at a limping pace, keeping Charles close.

※※※※ ※※※※

They kept going through the night. More creatures crossed their path, but Sym was able to keep them hidden. Only once more did Derek need to draw his blade.

As dawn approached, the mist grew thicker. Or perhaps it was their nearing the tower that caused the grey fog to intensify.

"Do you hear that?" Charles whispered as light began to pierce the edge of the horizon.

Derek froze. Sweat beaded down his forehead from the pain in his ankle. They'd stopped often enough to rest in the darkness, but it was getting worse.

A few seconds passed, and he shot a look at his brother. "I don't hear anything. Sym? Greggory?"

The sea witch shook her head, and Greggory did the same with a squeak.

"What is it, Charles?"

Charles's darker, more chiseled face hardened. His eyes narrowed. "It's the wizard. Has to be."

"Is he speaking to you?"

Charles snarled. "Not quite. He's saying a princess is waiting to be rescued. It's more of what the girl in the village heard. 'Charles, come save your princess.'" His hand clenched into a fist.

"That's good," Derek said. He tightened his grip on Charles's arm. "If he's still calling you, it means he doesn't know how close we are."

Sym raised an eyebrow at this, but Derek gave her a meaningful look, and she stayed silent.

"How close are we?" Charles's voice was tight.

"I can see the tree line," Sym murmured. "We're nearly there."

Chapter Twenty-Five

An Illusion

Riva rose before the sun. Her chest ached, throat sore from her fury the night before. She scoured the room again, searching for anything that might serve as a better weapon than her own hands.

She came up empty but found a coat in the wardrobe and pulled it on over her clothes. Then she went to the door. With grunting effort, she shoved the furniture out of the way.

The door was stuck.

Not stuck, Riva realized as she found the seam where the door closed. Rather, the wood had melded to the stone. Magic. Some twisted magic that sealed her in the top of the tower.

She slammed the wood with her palm, a fresh surge of frustration boiling in her veins. She stared at the door for a few seconds. Then she pulled her braid forward.

Riva flexed her hands, inhaling as determination filled her. She closed her eyes, feeling for the magic she knew was in her. The magic that was the reason she was taken. The reason her family had always viewed her as a problem rather than an asset.

She exhaled through her lips.

Warmth spread down her shoulder to her chest, sinking through the weight of her hair.

Riva put her palms on the door. Heat ran down her arms, through her fingertips, and up against the wood.

Her hands vibrated with the energy surging through them. But there was a barrier. Some force of magic stronger than her. It drew her power in. She tried to pull away, but her hands were stuck to the door.

It was feeding on her. Gadrel's magic, feeding on her power once more.

Riva gritted her teeth. With a snarl she broke the flow of her magic.

She staggered back as her palms were released. Anger roiled. Anger and exhaustion.

She was so tired of being furious. So tired of being used. So tired of being alone.

She turned from the door, flexing her hands and striding toward the balcony. Light glowed on the horizon to the east. Morning was coming quickly. With it, the danger that her love would trek through the forest and succumb to whatever spell Gadrel had cast on the mist.

Riva pulled open the balcony doors and stepped into the chilly air. She tugged the coat closed, fastening the silver buttons. Her lip curled.

Then her jaw dropped. On either side of the tower, more visible if she stuck her head out over the rail, were identical structures. Towers, stretched as high as the one she was in. Ivy growing up the sides, balconies matching hers', and figures... women on each balcony, identical as well, from the borrowed coat to the flowing golden hair stretching halfway down their towers.

Riva stumbled half a step back, horror and confusion roiling through her. Her stomach churned, and she pressed cold fingers to her lips.

Movement caught her gaze. People, approaching from the forest.

The churning in her stomach grew to bile in her throat. She recognized the dark shock of hair, the muscular build, and the cloak on Charles's broad shoulders. Tears welled in her eyes as he stepped into the clearing.

But something was wrong. More wrong than the duplicate towers and doppelgangers.

Her brow furrowed at the way Charles clutched the arm of one of his companions. His footsteps were faltering. His gaze remained straight ahead, not darting up to find her. She was sure she was visible, because the woman on his right was looking from each tower to the next, catching Riva's eye each time.

Her anxiety reached a breaking point.

"Charles!" Riva called out, her heart thudding in her chest.

On either side, the other women in the other towers did the same.

A heavy thud sounded below. Another chill ran through Riva's veins as Gadrel came into view, stalking toward the three companions with his cloak billowing behind him.

"I see you got my invitation," the wizard said, his voice echoing through the tower clearing.

Charles raised his chin. He still did not meet her eye, or even look in her direction.

What was wrong with him?

Riva's pulse raced. She scrambled back through the balcony doors and to the only other way out of the tower. The door was still sealed shut.

She slammed a fist against it. Nothing happened.

With a growl of frustration, Riva hurried to the table and hefted one of the heavy wooden chairs. She returned to the door and swung the chair with all her might.

It shattered against the wood. Splinters flew, her arms vibrated with the ricochet, and the door remained, impossibly, unscarred. Not so much as a scratch on the wooden surface.

With a muttered curse, Riva hurried back to the balcony.

The troop of three had come to a halt with several yards between themselves and Gadrel.

She thought she recognized the man beside Charles from descriptions he'd given in the past, but it didn't seem plausible that the crown prince of Cerulean would be there now. Not with how often Charles had spoken of how sheltered Prince Derek was.

The woman was new. Riva winced at the gashes marring her face, though they didn't seem to be distracting her from the approaching threat.

Her dark gaze flicked to Riva once more and to the women in the other towers. When she spoke, her words chilled Riva to the bone.

CHAPTER TWENTY-SIX

Hear the Difference

"This illusion magic is strong," Sym said. She didn't bother keeping her voice low. Instead, it took on that unnatural gravely tone that came when she tapped into her magic.

Charles swallowed. "What does that mean?" He tightened his grip on Derek's arm, and his brother returned the pressure. He'd heard Riva. Heard his love's voice echo three times over from three different directions. Each sounded as familiar as the last.

His sight was gone, but Derek had murmured the reality of the situation to him as they'd approached from the tree line. The triplicate towers and princesses. The trick created by the wizard in case they made it through the woods.

The ground had at least evened out. Charles managed his footsteps into the clearing, listening with all his might in the hope that he'd be able to tell his Riva from the imposters.

Fear gripped his heart. Fear that she might already be gone. That all of this might be an illusion.

"One of the towers is real," Sym replied. "One of the princesses, too. He is creating replicas. Duplicates of Riva that will act as she does but without the weight of reality behind them."

"I can't see them," Charles said through clenched teeth.

Footsteps padded ahead of them, and he heard the slip of Derek's sword from the sheath beside him.

Charles reached for his own hilt, his hand knowing the movement without need for sight.

"No."

Charles snarled at the voice. The same one which had sarcastically welcomed them when they'd entered the clearing. It was the wizard. It had to be.

"I don't suppose you can see them," the man said. "A pity; part of the spell wasted. Though I'm sure it confuses your companions. Even the witch can't tell them apart."

Sym gave a sharp intake of breath. Charles caught the sound of a faint, angry, squeak.

"You know what I am," Sym said, the calm in her voice at odds with the way her arm trembled beside his.

"Oh yes," the wizard drawled.

Charles grimaced at his haughty tone.

Derek shifted, keeping a hand on Charles's arm but putting a slight distance between them. Chilly morning air filled the space where he'd been.

"I thought I smelled rotting fish before we crossed the border. Though," he paused, and Charles thought he heard a smirk in the man's voice, "it seems you don't recognize me."

Sym's feet shuffled against the grass. The sound of her locks of twisted black hair softly thudding against her shoulders stirred even more anger in Charles. The wizard was taunting her.

"Should I?"

The man before them, standing still if the constant volume of his voice was to be trusted, chuckled.

Charles's hand tightened on his hilt.

"Too much salt water is not good for your mind, witch. Or perhaps you've been spending your own lifeforce, as I have."

"No." Sym's voice was sure and strong, a contrast to the nerves Charles felt in the air between them. "I'm not a fool. And I have no wish to destroy the land I call home. Unlike you, it seems. I may not remember *you*, but you've forgotten the oaths we all took. You're a *disgrace* to the world of magic."

A wave of heat followed her words. Not stemming from Sym, but from ahead of them. Charles shifted, his weight moving to the balls of his feet as he prepared to swing on whatever enemy was approaching.

"A spell," Derek murmured beside him. "Sym blocked it."

Indeed, as Charles listened, he heard the heavy breathing of the already magically drained sea witch.

"I was expecting a blind prince," the wizard called. Frustration was tight in his voice. "Not a little entourage. But no matter. I take it the rest of you haven't met the princess before?"

"Is that how it works, then?" Derek took a step forward, his hand still on Charles's arm, holding him back. "Someone who has *seen* Riva goes through the mist and then they're blind?"

"Not quite so simple in terms of spellcraft, but yes, that's the general idea."

Charles bristled at the wizard's condescending tone. The man had moved. His voice was to their left now, a few steps closer. Charles inhaled, focusing less on the words and more on the sounds around him.

His companions continued to breathe. The wind did as well, rushing in and out of the tower clearing. He could only guess how high the tower itself was. Riva was there, standing on one of the three identical balconies. If he listened... if he listened close enough, maybe he'd be able to tell them apart.

But he wouldn't get the chance if the wizard was not stopped.

"How tall is he?" Charles hissed. "What's his reach?"

"You stay here," Derek growled, his voice equally low. "You can't see."

Charles ignored that. "You know you blinded the girl?" he said loudly. "The maid who works for you? She's blind as well. Could have died in those woods."

A scoff. "She should have left sooner. If she didn't dawdle, she'd have been in the village by the time the spell took effect."

Charles shook his head. "I don't know if you deserve magic. I don't know if that's how magic works. But you certainly don't deserve an ounce of loyalty from those people." He practically spat the words. "How dare you be so *careless* about what happens to those in your charge."

Fury shook him, rattling the calm he usually felt before a battle.

He'd experienced a handful. Never a full fog of war, steel clashing against shield, fields wet with blood. But his ships had been boarded by pirates from time to time, and he'd defended more than a few travelers on the road when pillagers tried to make a bloody day's work.

"You have a chance," Derek called.

Charles bristled. Derek squeezed his arm.

"Give us the princess and renounce your claim on this land. Let the people in the village decide if they want to allow you to remain here."

What started as laughter from the wizard shifted as Derek spoke. It became a furious snarl, words spitting from the man's mouth as he retorted.

"You don't tell *me* what to do, boy. I've lived more lives than every member of your family combined. I've been on this land since before the whelps in Havita conceived the notion of settling here. I have the claim, the *right* to be here."

"You gave up that claim when you sucked the life from everything around you," Charles said. "Release Riva."

He felt movement beside him and almost flinched at Derek's whisper in his ear.

"I'm letting you go. I'll call his location from my end but use caution."

A thrum of nerves ran through Charles. He nodded.

"If you won't release the princess," Derek said, his voice gaining distance as his hand left Charles's arm. "We will have to free her ourselves."

"That girl has given me enough power to curse a forest... you think you can defeat me with that kind of magic running through my veins?"

Charles swallowed and drew his sword. "It's not a matter of thinking we can." He clicked his teeth, an image of Riva swimming to the front of his mind. "It's knowing we must."

Blood on the Grass

Derek made eye contact with Greggory just before the mouse scurried down Sym's arm and pantleg and into the grass. Good. The little guy didn't need to be in this fight.

Derek stepped away from Charles, his gut knotting at the idea of leaving his blinded brother but knowing from experience that staying clustered together was a horrible idea. Besides which, he needed to get closer to the wizard so he could provide a distraction for Sym.

She moved as well, her bare feet nearly silent on the grass as she circled the wizard from the other side.

Derek adjusted his grip on his short sword, then drew the dagger from his belt. With a weapon in each hand, he glanced up at each of the three towers.

"I'd come get you," he called. "But I have no idea which of you is the real one. Charles has spoken of you constantly, though. I'm eager to meet."

The woman in the tower to the left shrieked and cried out to be rescued. The ones in the middle and right let out barking laughs.

Derek grinned. That probably narrowed it down a bit. From everything Charles said, Riva was not the shrieking type.

He inhaled, cracked his neck, and strode across the grass toward the wizard. "Straight ahead, Charles."

His brother moved as well. His footsteps were slow at first, then faster as Gadrel yelped in surprise.

The brothers attacked at the same time.

Derek focused on his blades. He swung with his sword. Ducked, spun around, and stabbed up with the dagger. The blade caught a bit of flesh, blood dripping from Gadrel's thigh.

The man let out a grunt of pain.

On his other side, Charles had swung as well. His left fist connected with the wizard's chest, but his sword went wide.

Derek repositioned for another attack.

Gadrel slammed his palms together.

Both princes were blasted backward. The force of it knocked Derek off his feet and sent him sprawling onto the grass. His ankle twinged, the pain he'd pushed down flaring up again.

Across from him, Charles was already back on his feet, looking around with wild, unseeing eyes.

"Bit to the left," Derek called with a grimace.

Charles corrected and moved forward again, his head cocked to catch any trace of sound from Gadrel.

"I think not," the wizard spat. He waved his hand, murmuring some incantation as Charles charged forward.

The prince's sword hit, but not Gadrel. A shield of ice splintered into fragments as the force of Charles's attack knocked the wizard off center.

Behind him, Sym crept forward. Her hands rose in front of her, fingers twisting and twitching in complicated movements that hurt Derek's eyes before he looked away.

He scrambled to his feet as she neared the wizard.

"Charles, back," he shouted.

Charles dove backwards just as a ball of scorching energy slammed into Gadrel's back. The heat of it caressed Derek's skin, even from the distance he'd maintained.

To his disappointment, Gadrel simply shook his shoulders and turned to face Sym. Water dripped from his cloak. The shield of ice must have surrounded him entirely, catching the brunt of Sym's blast.

Charles hissed, patting blindly at his sleeve. Charred fabric smoked on his shoulder.

"Is he down?" he demanded.

"Not even a little," Gadrel scoffed. "Though your witch packs quite a bit of power. Maybe I'll add her to my collection." His voice grew quiet. "She'd keep me going for a *long* time."

He pulled a corded bag from his cloak and tossed it at Sym's feet.

The witch, already sweating from effort and drain, darted backward. But not quickly enough. The bag burst open upon impact. Vines, black and coated with thorns, erupted from the ground around Sym's feet. They twisted and wound up her legs.

She cried out as they constricted. Thick, sharp thorns stabbed into her, locking her to the spot.

Derek's vision went red. Rage bubbled in his gut, rising to his chest like steam from a kettle, heating every inch of him with trembling fury. He switched his grip on the dagger, sliding sideways and whipping it toward the wizard with as much force as he could muster.

The man caught sight of the blade just in time, ducking to the side as it soared past his head.

"You won't touch her," Derek growled, his voice low and dangerous. He shifted his grip, clutching the sword with two hands and swinging it over his head.

Gadrel raised an arm, and the blade sank into flesh.

The wizard screamed. A sound rich and justified to Derek's ears.

"Brother!" Charles charged forward, giving Derek just enough time to move aside as he swung toward the sound.

His blade found purchase as well.

They were close. Derek glanced past their foe. Sym's cracks had widened, black encroaching upon her features as she worked up another spell, hopefully one to rid herself of the vines. They'd ceased growing but extended up her legs to her mid-thigh.

Each time she moved, more blood coated the grass below her.

Fear clutched tight to Derek as he focused back on the wizard.

Gadrel pulled another item from his cloak. A small string of chains.

Derek set his stance, preparing to block whatever magic came his way.

Charles spun, his unseeing eyes closed as he tilted his head, listening.

Derek inhaled, another bout of fear blossoming in his chest at how close his brother was to Gadrel.

"Charles—"

The word barely left his lips before Gadrel's wrist flicked.

The chain grew impossibly fast. It whipped toward Charles, latched around his shoulders, and yanked him toward the wizard.

It all happened so fast. Derek lunged, then froze, a chill setting his hairs on end.

Charles was caught. The magical chain tightened around his torso, pressing his arms to his sides and squeezing so hard he dropped his sword.

And hovering at his neck, silver blade glinting in the morning light, was Gadrel's dagger.

CHAPTER TWENTY-EIGHT

Watching, Wishing, Wanting

Riva watched the fight below, heart in her throat, helpless frustration in every breath.

Each attack from the princes brought a bloom of hope to her chest. Each time Gadrel struck one of them back, she flinched as though the magic was attacking her. The woman was, indeed, a witch. A strong one, given the effort Gadrel was putting into the battle.

He'd attempted a handful of attacks on the men, each slipping off and around them as though the magic were water and the two of them had been dipped in oil.

She wanted to call out. To let Charles know she was there, watching, wishing, wanting him. But she knew better. She knew distraction in these moments could get him killed, and so she remained silent for the most part.

And then the witch was trapped. Riva's hand flew to her mouth in horror at the briars stabbing into her legs. The horror grew as a chain, glinting with silver runes, wrapped itself around Charles.

In the space of a breath, he was pulled to Gadrel, the wizard's blade held securely at his throat.

"*No!*" She screamed it. The sound reverberated through the clearing.

An echo of the anguish and fear within her sounded from the other two towers. So far from the true pain and terror she felt that it seemed impossible for someone to believe them.

Charles's brother turned and met her gaze. He dipped his chin in a nod, then refocused on Gadrel.

"Release him," Derek said. His voice carried high, reaching her on the balcony even as the wind swept through her skirts and coat.

She leaned over the edge, her hands bracing against the cold railing. It tingled, as though a surge of static moved through the iron.

"You have no leverage," Gadrel called out. He glanced toward Riva, and another shudder ripped down her spine. "No threat to use against me in this moment, boy. Do not *think* to give me orders."

He pressed the blade against Charles's skin, drawing a thin line of blood as the prince winced.

Riva sucked in a cold breath. "*Please.*"

Derek turned to glance up again. His jaw was tight.

Riva clenched the rail, her knuckles going white as she stared down at the wizard. "Please," she called again. "Release him. You can have my name. My power. Just release him. Let them live."

Gadrel craned his neck up at her. "You want to cooperate *now*? Now that your little friends have injured me? Have driven dangerous thoughts into the minds of my servants? Have brought a *witch* to my home?"

"I would cooperate," she replied, her voice shaking. "If you let them go. I will."

His lip curled, the sneer digging a fresh pit of disgust and anger in Riva's stomach. At the same time, a familiar heat surged in her chest. Her hair shifted, caught in the wind as it loosened from its bindings.

"Don't."

Riva's eyes widened. Her breath came sharp and shallow at the strangled sound of Charles's voice.

He didn't look—couldn't, she realized as his eyes flicked blindly in her direction. But he spoke, the movement of his jaw causing Gadrel's blade to dig deeper into his skin.

"Don't do what he wants, Riva."

Tears pooled in her eyes at his words. Her lips trembled. She shifted, climbing atop the rail and clutching one of the tall pillars that maintained the overhang.

"Bravery, prince?" Gadrel's voice dripped with disdain. "That will get you nowhere in this world." He glanced up at Riva. "You swear it? On *his* life? You swear to obey me if I release him?"

"All of them," Riva corrected, clenching her teeth to stop the trembling. Her hand balled into a fist at her side. In her peripheral vision, streaming locks of golden hair caught the breeze. "You let all of them leave, unharmed, and I will swear it."

"No." Gadrel sneered. "You swear it now, or I kill him where he stands."

"You kill him, and you'll die before his body falls." Derek took a furious half-step toward them.

Riva swallowed, her fear and fury mingling with the warmth still growing in her chest.

"We are at an impasse," Gadrel said mildly. He looked from Derek to Riva. "I expect nothing but confusion and foolishness from young royal pups. You weren't overly difficult to control these last few days, princess. I see no reason to take up your offer when I can simply slit this boy's throat and then re-make your cuffs."

"That's all right," Riva called down.

The wizard's face scrunched in confusion, his blade dipping half an inch as he cocked his head at her.

"I was lying anyway."

And she jumped.

⁂

Riva closed her eyes as she released the pillar. Her inhale brought another rush of warmth to her body. Heat traveled her veins, filled her lungs, and pooled at the center of her. Like a core of molten glass ready to be formed into a work of art.

And form it, she did.

Her hair glowed in ribbons of gold behind her. It feathered out, slowing her descent. But not too much. She needed to reach Gadrel before his shock wore off.

He gaped, like a fish out of water, as she tore through the sky towards him. His grip loosened, and Charles made to dart away.

Gadrel snarled, snatched the chain still tight around Charles's torso, and pulled him back.

She was halfway there. Everything moved in distorted, slow-motion. With a flick of her wrist, a strand of gold whipped toward the prince and the wizard. It snapped like a whip, leaving a shiny red slash across Gadrel's hand.

He released the chain with a howl of pain.

She sent another tendril of magic toward his other hand, the one holding the blade. Then another and another.

Half a dozen welts spread across his skin where Riva's power met him.

He dropped the blade.

It hit the ground the same time as Riva's feet. She stumbled on the grass, tumbling to her knees with a grunt. The fall was not detrimental. Nor was it slow enough for a graceful landing.

She raised her head just as a shadow crossed her path and warm hands found her face.

"Riva." Charles's relief sounded in the breaking of his voice. He ran his hands over her face, to her shoulders, down her arms, clenching one of her hands with his and moving his other back to her cheek. "You're alive... you're all right?"

She almost couldn't speak. Power still thrummed through her, overwhelming her every breath. She exhaled, urging her hair to calm. Then she lifted her free hand and caressed Charles's brawny features.

"I'm all right. And you..."

He nodded, those dark eyes filling with tears even as they didn't quite meet hers. "I'll be fine. I just wish I could see your face."

A roar of rage brought their situation back into sharp focus. Riva jerked backward, attempting to put her body in front of Charles's. He did the same, and the two ended up shoulder to shoulder on their knees, hands still clenched tight.

The wizard faced them, the welts gone from his hands, and the youth gone from his face. He'd aged well past what Riva had seen before. Canyons of wrinkles showed every scowl and frown he'd ever worn. His hair was gone at the top, fading from grey to white around his ears.

Magic balled in each of his palms. Pure, raw energy that crackled with heat.

Riva's hair floated, bouncing on her shoulders almost as though she were underwater. She didn't need its warning. Gadrel wanted them dead.

"You—" Gadrel's voice broke off with a horrid squelching sound. He stooped forward, body bending around the point of a sword protruding from his stomach. The magic fell from his hands. It scorched the ground on either side of him, holes burning through the grass and dirt as plumes of acrid smoke framed his features.

Riva winced, but her focus was drawn not to the wizard but the prince standing behind him.

Derek's gaze was fixed on his brother, fear painted into the intensity of his gaze and the furrow of his brow.

Silence encompassed them. The faint sizzling of Gadrel's power, still eating away at the ground on either side of him, and the low hiss of his final breath leaving his lungs were the only sounds to break the quiet.

Derek pulled out his blade. And the wizard fell.

CHAPTER TWENTY-NINE

Advice of a Sea Witch

Faint squeaking and nibbling broke through the haze of sound Charles was still trying to decipher.

Riva's voice, that voice he'd been so terrified of never hearing again, spoke beside him. "You can't see?"

Charles turned her direction, his hand still clenching tight to her. "No. It was that mist. I don't know..."

He blinked.

It was slow, the shift from darkness to light, but as he blinked again and shook his head to clear it, shapes permeated his sight.

"He's gone." Sym's sharp voice, tight with pain, sounded a good distance from him. "His magic will be fading as well."

Familiar fingers caressed Charles's face. They pushed a lock of hair from his forehead. Heat moved across his skin. Breath, uneven and shaky and hot, just beside his lips.

He leaned forward, tilting his head.

His lips met Riva's and locked into place like the gears of an intricate clock. He dove into the soft warmth of her. Drowning by choice as her hands enveloped him, her heat and passion only matched by his own.

Their embrace was interrupted by a distinct series of short coughs from Derek.

Charles pulled back, laughter bubbling up as he caught sight of his brother trying to look anywhere but at the two lovers.

Then he blinked. "I can…"

"Yes, yes," Sym said with haughty indifference. "True love's kiss will obviously speed things along. Now, these vines are going to take a good long while to melt away. So, if someone besides little Greggory could give me a hand?"

It was difficult not to continue laughing, though the sight of the blood on the sea witch's legs sobered much of Charles's humor.

He rose, still clutching Riva's hand, and drew her with him to standing. Derek rushed to Sym's side, and while Charles was concerned, he also knew the witch well enough by now to know she did not require additional assistance.

Not with Greggory still gnawing at the vines with his sharp little teeth.

Instead, Charles turned to Riva.

She gaped at him, the disbelief in her eyes almost heart-breaking.

"I'm here," he murmured. He reached up, shifting one of her impossibly long strands of hair behind her ear. "I'm here, Riva. Are you... are you all right?"

She opened her mouth and, rather than words, a weak chuckle escaped. Then she swallowed. "I think I am. I didn't..." She swallowed and, with her free hand, ran fingers through her golden hair. "I didn't know I could do that."

"Of course not," Sym snapped. "How could you have any inkling of what your magic can do with a life of constant sheltering and no proper teacher?"

Charles pinched his lips together. The adrenaline of battle, the return of his sight, the reunion with his love... amusement didn't seem as though it should have been the appropriate response, but he required every ounce of self-control to not burst out laughing again.

"Perhaps we give them a moment, Sym?" Derek asked, both amusement and exhaustion lining his words.

Charles heard Sym's grumbled "very well then" as he and Riva moved a few paces from the slain wizard's body.

"I came as soon as I heard," Charles said, gazing into Riva's eyes.

Her usually bright smile was muted, worn and tired, which was to be expected. But he also worried some part of her would be angry with him for taking so long to reach her.

"I know." Her hand returned to his cheek.

"I have so much to tell you," he murmured. Yet he found himself lost for words. Enveloped in relief, it was difficult to find the importance behind the things he needed to say.

"We can talk later," Riva said. "Back to the village?"

She turned, her gaze darting to the body on the ground before she looked at Derek and Sym.

"I'd like to meet your brother. And your friend." She frowned up at him. "How did he manage to get away? After what happened last time, I thought your father had the palace on lock down?"

Charles cleared his throat with a little cough. "About that... there is something that is perhaps more important than the rest that I should fill you in on."

Riva raised an eyebrow. "Does it have something to do with the magic your friend possesses?"

"You could say that." Charles nodded with a chuckle. "The last letter you received from me was sent right before a number of *very* strange things happened."

Riva hesitated a moment, and Charles worried he was overwhelming her. Then she walked, pulling him along with her, toward Derek and Sym.

The sea witch had finally been freed from the vines. The dark plants lay withered and slashed on the grass. She and Derek were each spreading palmfuls of poultice over the wounds on her legs.

Greggory helped.

"Can we help?" Riva asked.

"No, about done now," Derek replied. He stood with a grunt, favoring his ankle, and wiped his hands across his trousers.

"Are you all right?" Riva looked at Sym.

Charles squeezed her hand, grateful for her making eye contact with the witch rather than staring at the many large black cracks in her skin.

"I'll manage. Not the first time a wizard has thought himself high and mighty around me. If we were nearer the sea…" She grimaced.

Derek put a hand on her shoulder. "You were brilliant. We'd be dead without you half a dozen times over."

"Well, I know that." Sym rolled her eyes.

Riva cackled with laughter, earning an appraising look from the witch.

"I'm starving," Riva said to the lot of them.

Sym grinned, showing her rows of inhumanly sharp teeth. "As am I, princess."

"Riva, please." Riva reached out with her free hand, still holding tight to Charles with the other, and clasped Sym's arm. "And thank you."

Sym's eyes went wide for a brief second. Then she swallowed and nodded. She turned to Derek. "Food."

"The inn?" Derek asked with a glance at Charles.

"Yes." Charles nodded. "We ought to fill them in on what happened anyway."

Sym strode a few paces away and nudged the wizard's body with her bare foot. "Perhaps not the specifics of *everything* that happened." She looked at Riva. "If you'd hear the advice of a sea witch, princ—Riva."

Riva inclined her head.

"I suggest you keep the scope of your power to yourself for the time being. Cerulean has not had a witch queen in over six hundred years. The court will find it quite odd."

Charles was not entirely prepared for the expression on Riva's face as she turned to look at him. Her eyebrows were raised with incredulity, her lips opened in half a question, half exasperation.

"What, exactly, happened between your last letter and now?"

CHAPTER THIRTY

Brothers

Derek pressed a hand to his hair. It had been a long time since he'd spent more than a few minutes getting it how he liked. But today was different. He needed to look presentable, sharp, everything the best man and second-in-line to the throne should be for the crown prince's wedding.

He cast a glance at Charles. His brother, no longer little but always that way in his mind, beamed with a smile so bright the vast windows in the great hall were unnecessary. Evening sun shone through them, but the myriad of colors it cast against the golden pillars were nothing compared to the light in Charles's eyes as he caught sight of Riva entering through the grand double-doors.

The wedding plans had gone quickly. Upon the return of their little party to Lagonia, the king had agreed to overlook Charles's daring escapade, and Derek's involvement in said adventure, if they ensured a marriage within the month.

Invitations were sent. Riva's family was alerted—though Derek privately thought they should have waited until after the marriage to inform them. Half the royal court of Cerulean showed up for the pre-wedding dinners and weeklong celebrations in the capital city. The rest had arrived the night before.

The palace was full to bursting.

Sym was back to her normal, incredibly odd, self. Derek was almost certain she'd jumped off the ship on their way home. He'd lost sight of her for a bit, and when she'd returned her skin had glistened with saltwater, the cracks lining her face had shrunk considerably, and her off-putting smile had been back in place.

She used some kind of illusion at the moment, standing across from him on the dais. A larger woman stood beside her, both dressed in stunning gowns of ruby red lined with golden accents. Sym looked almost normal, though the ethereal beauty of her essence still permeated the room, drawing many eyes before the princess entered.

Riva strode forward at a purposeful pace. King Victor walked alongside her, recovering quickly from his startled expression at her speed. The court would talk for nearly a week of how the princess couldn't wait to marry Charles and practically dragged the king to the altar in her hurry.

Her gown of white was offset with ruby and gold designs. The embroidery matched the many jewels beaded into her long hair. Half of her golden locks were pinned up in a stunning design of intricate braids. The rest hung nearly as long as the train of her dress.

Music drowned the sound of their footsteps. Soft and romantic, it sent a delightful shiver down Derek's spine as he watched Charles's eyes well with tears.

"Keep it together, brother," Derek whispered. "You're almost there."

Charles turned and met Derek's gaze. They shared a nod, a moment of understanding.

"Thank you," Charles replied, before putting his full attention on his bride.

The younger princes and princesses sat through the ceremony rather well. Derek made a mental note to check in with them during the reception. There would be plenty of time. He and Sym had already discussed their plans. They'd stay in Lagonia for a bit. Sym needed to be near the sea, and Derek needed to be near his family.

Beyond Sym's desire to rest on the coast, was her promise to teach Riva. The young princess had discovered a power greater than she imagined. Her love for Charles had given her a modicum of control in that moment on the tower, but living with the magic she possessed would require rigorous training.

Once things settled, once the nobility returned to their estates, scattered across Cerulean, Derek and Charles would discuss a handful of the troubling things they'd each witnessed on their individual adventures.

They'd list out what needed to be solved first. They'd talk to the king. And slowly, a bit at a time, they'd continue their mother's work of making Cerulean the finest, and fairest, kingdom of them all.

Derek was glad to be home, but part of him already itched to be back on the road. That life, those next adventures, would come in time.

He clapped his hands together as the king finalized the young couple's oaths. Applause filled the great hall as Charles and Riva shared another kiss, this one more restrained than the one which had returned his sight under the tower.

Across from him, clapping her hands together with equal happiness on her face, Sym met his gaze. A crooked smile turned up one of her cheeks, and the little mouse on her shoulder gave Derek a wave.

He waved back.

Acknowledgements

Thank you to everyone who loved Song of the Deep enough to convince me to keep writing The Old Tales. I am so excited to explore this world of fairy and folk tales.

Please consider leaving a review for Song of the Deep and A Voice in the Tower! Reviews are a huge help for authors, indie authors especially.

Find all my works as well as my newsletter and goodies at chlyn.com!